One Handed Reads Series, #1-3

Dee Lish

Teased

Chapter One

She stands in front of me, dressed in a sexy little feminine outfit that makes me wet almost instantly. Black heels over white stockings, which I know from experience means that she's also wearing white lace suspenders, bra, and knickers. She has a cute little black floral cotton skater dress over the top. Her makeup is perfect; long fake eyelashes, and ruby-red lips, which are currently greeting me with a seductive smirk. Her hair is in a cute little bob, just skimming her shoulders. Neat as always. My girl is, to me, walking perfection.

"You're wearing too many clothes," she remarks. "You know I like you naked when we're together."

I stand and begin to remove my clothing. I don't waste any time, pulling off my knickers with my leggings. My bra and top disappear soon after that. "Happy now?" I grin at her, holding my hands out to my sides, letting her enjoy every inch of my nude form.

"Come here," she demands and moves towards me, grabbing me at the back of my neck and pulling me tight against her. She cups my face in her hands, and my hands instinctively move around her waist. Quickly, her lips descend on mine, her tongue pushing into my mouth with force, demanding I accept.

I gladly take her tongue into my mouth, lapping at it with mine before sucking on it gently. A soft moan greets my actions and my fingers dig into her hips as my desire builds, increasing the wetness between my legs.

She lets one hand stray down over my bare skin as she kisses me. She cups a tit in her hand and rolls my nipple between her thumb and forefinger, making it my turn to moan against her mouth.

Her hand strays further, skimming over my hips and stomach before reaching its ultimate goal between my legs. She pushes her finger between my labia, my arousal ensuring she meets no resistance before her digit grazes my clit. I groan, my hips involuntarily pushing back against her hand.

"Always ready for me, aren't you?" she breathes against my lips as she breaks our kiss. "You're such a whore."

I know name-calling probably shouldn't turn me on, but it does.

She lifts her hand away from my pussy and rubs her fingers over my lips. Instinctively, I run my tongue over the wet trail she leaves, and she seizes the opportunity to direct me to suck her fingers clean of my pussy juices.

Tasting myself on her fingers just increases my need. I suck on them hungrily, and she laughs. "Good girl. You clean my fingers. Suck them like you will my cock."

My pulse quickens at the thought of her using her strap-on with me, but before I get the chance to think about it too hard, she puts her hand on my shoulder and pushes me. I drop to my knees and she puts her foot forward in my direction.

"Kiss it," she demands, and I sink to my hands and knees and lean forward to kiss her foot. I know she's not about the dominance of the act. My girl just likes to perv on my arse in the air while I kiss her feet. I give it a peck and look up at her.

"You can do better than that," she says, and I run my tongue over her shoe and the top of her foot in long, lavish strokes.

"Good girl." She grins down at me, knowing full well what effect calling me that has on me. When she's satisfied that I've paid enough attention to both feet, she tells me to turn from her, touch my nose to the floor, and keep my arse up in the air.

I eagerly await what she's going to do to me next when I feel a cold dribble of lubricant run over my asshole. Just enough not to cause damage, but definitely not enough to be anything but painfully aware of what she's doing.

The tip of something is pressed against my asshole, and I wait as she slides the butt plug deep inside without too much concern for my comfort. She gives me a good, hard smack on the arse, making sure to slap the base of the plug in the process. She strokes over my arse and slips her fingers back between my legs, teasing my clit again, making me move against her hand. I want to come, already so full of need. Just before I get to that point, she pulls her hand away, and I groan in frustration.

"Get on the bed, on your back, and lean your head right on the edge," she tells me.

I do as I'm told. She turns to face away from me, then backs towards me and straddles my head. She lowers herself to my face before covering me with her lace-covered cunt.

"Lick me," she demands.

I move my tongue against her knickers, seeking out her

cunt and working my mouth against her, teasing her, making sure I have her just as aroused as she has me.

I hook my tongue past her knickers, making contact with her skin, and lick along her now exposed cunt, running my tongue around her entrance before fucking into her. She grinds against my face and moans her satisfaction. I grab her thighs with my hands and keep her pulled tight against my face. I can barely breathe and it makes me dizzy, but that only turns me on even more. I need to make her come so badly, and she knows it.

She breaks our contact and stand, then turns to face me. "Drop your head back off the bed a little more."

I do as I'm told. Once there, I'm greeted with a full view of what she has in mind for me. Knowing I'm watching her every move, she lifts her dress slowly and pulls down the front of her knickers, revealing the big, hard strap-on she had tucked away this whole time.

"Hands over your head," she tells me and straddles my head and arms. "Open your mouth."

When I do, she dips her hips, slips the head of her cock between my lips, and then leans over the length of my body, supporting her weight on either side of my legs.

I know what's coming, and between this and the burning stretch my arse has had, I'm on fire, my cunt is slick, and all I want is what she has to give me.

She starts to thrust gentle little strokes into my mouth, allowing me the time to build up my greed. I lie there, a gloriously sexy stocking-covered thigh against each arm on either side of my face, and her cock getting deeper and deeper with each slow, teasing thrust. I'm greedy for her, though. I need more and push my face up towards her with each movement from her hips. She stops and withdraws completely so she can look down at me.

"You want it all?" she asks, and I nod. She looks down at me, lifts her dress again, and watches as she slowly slides her cock into my mouth.

I breathe through my nose and try to keep relaxed as she hits the back of my throat and stops, the balls of her strap-on resting against my nose.

"Jesus," she says breathlessly, looking down at me with all of her cock in my mouth. My gag reflex kicks in and she pulls out again. She quickly leans back over me and starts a fiercer fucking of my face, brutally thrusting into my mouth like she would my cunt, filling me with her cock.

She leans on me, her hand between my legs. I spread them to allow her access, and she sinks two fingers deep into my sopping cunt. I moan around her dick and move my arms to grab at her ass and pull her harder into my throat. The more I take in my mouth, the more she plays with my cunt until I can't take it anymore, and I scream out in climax with her dick firmly between my lips.

She pulls the strap-on from my mouth and slaps my tits.

"Get on your knees," she demands.

I move slowly, still basking in the post-orgasmic bliss. and get on all fours. She climbs onto the bed behind me and shoves my face to the mattress. "Ass up, good girl," she teases.

I feel her hands on the butt plug, and she pulls it from my ass, dropping it to the floor. Quickly, she takes her cock and pushes it against my arsehole before pushing it hard into me. I cry out as she stretches my arse out with her dick, pushing it into me until she's balls deep in my poor little arse. My cunt throbs with need, and I groan and start to shift against her.

I can't help but think of how this must look, me completely naked, while she's still dressed perfectly, taking me hard in my greedy arse with a big fat cock. She pounds my ass without mercy until the need to come again rises in me. She spanks me hard as she pounds into me, and I come apart with her buried deep in my arse. I scream out, pushing back against her, needing to feel every last inch of her dick inside me. Then I feel it; her cock empties into me, filling me with cum. My hips give way, and she collapses on top of me, both of us panting, her cock still firmly inside me.

I know my place. Naked and at the ruthless mercy of my girl.

Chapter Two

I love stretching out in the passenger side of his black BMW 3 Series. There's just something about being in his company that I find utterly intoxicating. From the second I'm in the same space as him, a calmness falls over me. The knowledge that, in that moment, I'm exactly where I should be. Maybe it's the extent of my feelings for him or just his strong, manly presence. Something about his broad shoulders and tall stature that generate that flush of serenity. Whatever it is, at those times, I am content to be nowhere else in the world.

Miles pass, idle chitchat fades, and his closeness takes over. My pussy gets wetter, my nipples stiffen, and my breasts ache to be in his firm grip. But we have a long drive ahead of us, and it's going to be a while before that will be possible.

More miles sail past outside and the atmosphere inside the car is slowly charging with sexual electricity. I feel his eyes keep scanning over me, and I glance at him.

"All right?" he asks before returning his eyes to the road.

"Yeah, I'm all good," I reply. "I just need to be naked with you, and sooner rather than later."

That delicious smirk he has flashes across his mouth, and a sly sideways glance is shot in my direction.

"Good." He grins.

"Not good," I reply. "I'm already wet and horny."

Another look is shot in my direction. "You can wait," he tells me with more of a smirk.

I return it with a cheeky look on my face. "I don't really have to," I tell him. "I'm not the one driving." I reach for the seat controls, leaning back, getting myself some more space while still wearing my seatbelt.

My hands cup my breasts and give them a small squeeze. His eyes flick over to me and back to the road. "Keep driving, mister," I warn him, and slide my hands up underneath my top.

"Stop distracting me, then. It's dangerous!"

My hands roam over my tits under my clothes. My nipples pebble, and I can't resist the temptation of pulling on my bra and letting my breasts pop out, so I can get more access to my aching tits.

"Jesus," he says from the driver's seat.

"Keep your eyes on the road," I tell him, a sexual sigh following as I roll my nipples between my thumb and forefinger.

"Jen, if we have an accident, it's all your fault," he growls as he shifts uncomfortably in his seat. I can tell by how he moves that he's already hard for me. *Good. Let him suffer a little.*

My fingers vary between rolling my nipples with my thumb and grazing them with my fingertips, circling them, letting my nerve endings sizzle, my pussy getting wetter. Soft sighs and moans bubble up within me.

"Fuck," comes the curse of frustration from beside me.

"Mmmm," I hum breathlessly.

"Don't do it," he warns.

"I can't. Only you make me come with just my nipples being played with. For that, I need to do this..." I slide a hand into my leggings and slip it under my knickers, finding my pussy swollen and soaked.

I waste no time in spreading my legs as best I can in the front of his car and seeking out my clit.

"Mmmm, fuck," I hiss when my fingertip first caresses that sensitive little bundle of nerves.

"Christ," he groans beside me. "You're making it practically impossible to concentrate on the road."

I couldn't reply even if I wanted to. I'm already too focussed on the circling motion as I run my fingers over my clit, tempting and teasing myself onwards to the inevitable.

My heart speeds and my breathing gets quicker and shallower, my hand moves faster, and I know his eyes are boring holes into me. That knowledge makes my skin prickle with excitement, heightening the sensation that's building in my pussy.

I can feel my climax coming from the thrill of being in the car as it travels along where anyone from a higher vehicle can see what I'm doing. I know he's looking at me more than the road. I know this will be in his mind anytime he thinks of me in the car now too.

Before I know it, a powerful orgasm slams into me. I cry out loudly. Every muscle in my body tenses and colours decorate the backs of my closed eyelids. He pulls my hand from my leggings, and when my eyes finally open, he's putting my soaked fingertips into his mouth.

"Fuck," he sighs, as he lets his tongue trace over my fingers, tasting my juices. "You're going to pay for this later."

His voice is laced with lust. "I think my dirty girl needs a good spanking." He sucks on my index finger. "But first I'm going to fuck you the second we get to the hotel. You need it. Hard."

My pussy clenches and soaks even more.

As usual, I tease him, and he ends up being the one to drive me even more crazy. I should learn this each time, but I think that might be the real thrill in this little car sexcapade. No matter how much I tease him, he will always come back with the upper hand. And that's just how I like it.

Chapter Three

I finally make it out of the airport. He gets out of the car when he sees me, and when I get to him, he pulls me close against him for a hug. I revel in that contact, his arms around me, holding me tight.

"Hello, you," I breathe out against his ear. His lips meet mine, and I melt in against him, welcoming his tongue with mine. It's all I need to tell him in that moment. *Hello. I've missed you. I can't wait to have you alone.* Once our hellos have been said sufficiently, he grabs my case and throws it into the boot before we each head for our own side of his car. We pass the time with the usual idle chitchat. How was the flight? How's work? Until we're finally out on a main road and heading away from the airport.

When he leaves his hand resting on the gear stick, I take the opportunity to put my hand over it and guide it between my legs. I make sure to grind his hand in against what I'm trying to show him.

"Do you feel that?" I grin. He glances over at me and I know that look on his face all too well.

A small, cheeky smirk flashes across his lips. "I think you know what's going to happen to you once we've checked in."

I smirk back and let him think about what's going to happen for the rest of the short journey to the hotel. I watch the scenery pass by and flick through the music on his stereo.

I grab my case from the boot and make my way to reception to talk nicely to the man arranging my room key. Since he's standing beside me, I let my hand drop from the counter as I tap in my debit card PIN with the other hand. I let it rest against his crotch before applying a little pressure and rubbing against his cock that's trapped behind his jeans. I smile sweetly at the clerk, releasing my hand from him and taking the room key with it. I turn and head to the lift, letting him follow.

Nothing else is said until we get to the room. I dump my case and move back towards him. I push him hard against the wall and, again, my hand goes to his cock. My other hand grabs his and places it firmly over my strap-on. I rub over his length.

"I'm going to have this later. But first…" I pause, making him rub my own length, "…you're going to have this." I grin.

Hooded lids cover lust-filled eyes as his mouth descends on mine again. His arousal at the whole idea is oh-so-very apparent.

He kisses me hard, and again, my body moulds against his, responding to him in every way possible. I pull back from him and lead him by the hand, steering him over to the other side of the bed on the opposite side of the room. I circle him, running my hands leisurely over him through his t-shirt. Once at his rear, I pull one hand behind his back and guide it down to my strap-on. I encourage him to rub me, letting him stroke me like he would if it was a real dick. While he's enjoying that feeling, I slip my hand over his cock and rub it hard.

I grab his other hand and repeat the action, letting both of his hands roam over my strap-on, making friends with my cock before I make him intimately acquainted with it. I wrap my arms around him and pull his back against my front, my hands slipping under his t-shirt and running my fingers over his stomach and up over his chest. My fingertips focus on their goal of his nipples, and I graze them with my nails.

"I'm going to give you my cock, and there's not a damn thing you can do to stop me, is there?" I tease him.

A moan rumbles in his chest, and his fingers flex against my cock. "I guess not."

I run my hands back down over his skin, towards his waistband. I undo the button on the top of his jeans and glide the zip down. I push his legs apart with my foot and let his jeans slide to the floor. I follow them, making sure they are pooled at his ankles. As I rise back up, I run my hands over the outside of his legs before running them over his crotch when I stand up straight again.

His hard dick bobs in my hand in response to my touch. "Awww, you're so hard for a man who is about to get taken hard up the arse," I tease against his back.

"Oh, fuck!"

I grab the waistband of his boxers and pull them down to join his jeans. I repeat the action of running my hands up over his legs, only this time, when I finally stand up, I run my hands over his arse and let my finger slip along the valley between his buttocks.

I push him hard, and he falls face-first to the bed, bending at the waist to try to stop his feet from leaving the floor. When he does, it just allows me more access to his arse, and I don't stop pushing until he's resting against the top of the bed. I pull the lube from my jeans pocket and spread it over my fingers, then slip it back into my pocket and return my now lubed-up hand to his ass crack.

"Spread your damn legs, whore," I bark at him. "I can't exactly make you my little bitch if you aren't going to spread your legs for me." I smack my other hand down hard on his bare buttock, and he opens his legs wider.

I rub my fingers over his semi-exposed asshole, pushing against it, needing to be inside him already. I feel him attempting to relax around my first two fingers as I penetrate his slutty, tight little arse. He feels amazing around my digits, and I let them slip in and out of him, stretching him, lubing him up, ready for my dick. He moans again and pushes back against me, and I can't resist slipping a third digit into his arse.

The experience is making me wet as hell. The sounds he's making, the way his arse rises to meet every thrust of my fingers, the delicious tightness of him, and how amazingly filthy he likes to be is a heady combination that has me longing for more. I need to both sink my cock into him and have him sink his cock into me. Plenty of time for that later, though. For now, I'm thoroughly turned on by having him take my fingers into him.

The temptation is just too much, and when I let my fingers slide from his ass this time, I move slightly to the side of him so he can see me as he's bent over the bed. I lift my fingers to my lips and suck on every lubed-up one of them. He sucks in air as he watches me.

"I couldn't resist licking my fingers. I needed to taste

you," I say with a smirk, and the moan he breathes out tells me all I need to know.

I move back in behind him, placing a hand on each buttock and pulling them apart before I bury my face between them, my tongue seeking out his ass. I lick my way around that tight little ring of muscle before pushing my tongue into him, teasing him, encouraging more amazing noises from him, and I rim and tongue fuck his delicious arse.

I grab his buttocks harder, my nails biting into his flesh, needing more of him as I grind my face and tongue against his ass and tight little hole. I relish in the feel of him against me, delighting in the appreciative sounds and sighs he's letting out, feeling the slickness of my pussy against my thighs, knowing it's not enough. I need to have my cock buried inside him so I can feel the base of it pressing against my clit with every thrust into him I give.

My tongue trails up the entire length of his ass crack, and I move back with a short sharp crack of my right hand against his buttock. I pull the lube out of my jeans pocket again before making fast work of pulling my jeans and the boxers that I bought to wear while I had my cock on to the floor. Stroking my faux cock in my hand, I flip the lid on the lube and rub it over my length. I squirt a substantial amount on the head of my dick and let a sizable drop trickle down to his arsehole.

I push forward, holding my cock at his ass, pushing the head in firmly.

He lets out a long groan as his ass takes me inside. "Oh, fuck, yes," he pants, and I begin slow, shallow thrusts, each time teasing in a little deeper.

I keep up the pace, needing to be deeper inside him, not stopping until my false balls touch him. Once he has me deep, I take even more delight in pulling out and slamming back into him. He groans with every stroke, his ass rising to meet me, pushing back on my length, needing it just as much as I do.

"You like that, don't you?" I tease him. When he doesn't reply, I slam into him, making him grunt sexually. "I can't hear you, bitch. What did you say?"

"Jesus, YES!" he breathes.

I grab his hips and drive into him harder. I need to make sure he knows just who owns his ass; to make sure he's left with the feeling that I've been deep inside him for days afterwards. The pressure on my clit with every thrust just keeps driving me on. My own climax starts to build, and I'm craving it more than anything right now. I pound his arse furiously, needing to come.

"Fuck, your ass feels so good. God, you're such a whore, taking my dick so well. You're just such a fucking slut!" I taunt him again. "Tell me what you are!" I spank my hand down on his right buttock.

"Ohhh, fuck," he moans. "I'm your slut."

"Whose slut?" I ask, grinding against him while fully embedded up his arse.

A sharp exhale of breath makes me grin, and he moans, "Yours. Oh, fuck. I'm your whore!" I grin at his reply and sigh, my head falling back and my eyes closing as I savour every delicious feeling this is generating in me.

His moans of lust grow louder. He's pushing back on me with every stroke. My own sighs of pleasure start to mix with his, and I just can't help but keep driving on. Everything becomes one long sound of ass fucking between us. His groans, my moans, and the sound of my body slapping against his ass as I slam into him again and again. The pressure builds inside me, and heat pools in my lower stomach. I slam into him in sharp, fast, staccato strokes until my climax slams into me.

"Ohhh, fuck, yes!" I cry out as I come hard.

I can't stop. I don't want to. The sounds he's making are all too delicious, and I can't help myself. I keep pushing into him, forcing my cock as deeply as he can take it, making sure he knows I own his tender little arse completely. He's my little bitch. I reach around him and touch his balls, cupping them.

"Oh, Jesus!" he moans loudly. My hand grips his cock firmly. I need him to come; I need him to make a mess of himself, to really know what a glorious little anal whore he can be for me.

I let the movement of my thrusts force his cock through the tight grasp of my hand, caressing him with every stroke in his arse, driving him forward to climax. My own orgasm is already building within me once more.

"Tell me what you are!" I demand.

He moans again, backing against me as I thrust into his arse. I drive into him hard to get his attention. "I said, TELL ME WHAT YOU ARE!" I demand again.

"Oh, God! I'm a dirty little queer," he breathes.

"Who owns your whore ass?" I ask.

"You!" he cries out, his unsteady breathing telling me just how close he is. "You! I'm your anal slut. Jesus, you fill my ass so good."

Those words are my undoing for a second time. I come harder than before, still thrusting and letting those thrusts guide his cock through my grip. He twitches, bucking against my cock and hand in equal need, and with a loud groan, he explodes in a climax. His knees give way and I pull out of him. I move to his face, his open mouth panting still, and I press my cock against his lips.

"Suck it," I demand. "Taste your ass on my cock."

His lips part more and his tongue snakes out to the underside of my big fake dick. Christ, there is nothing more delicious than this man being a filthy little slut for me, and I will never tire of putting him in his place.

Chapter Four

I lie on the hotel room bed, making myself comfortable as I wait for her to appear from the bathroom. The room has a nice, comfortable king-sized bed, and I kick off my shoes, relax, and grab the TV remote, flicking through the channels while I wait.

When she finally walks out of the bathroom, I'm enthralled with what I see. She's standing there before me with a gag in her mouth, her nipples peeping out over the top of a black and red lacy corset. They're clamped, a little silver chain linking them. She has stockings, heels, and suspenders on, and on her ankles and wrists are leather restraints.

She's got a paper luggage label hanging from one of her nipple clamps. Just looking at her like this already has me hard. I get up, move around the bed to her, and take her little label in my hand to read it.

Yours to do whatever you wish with. Plugged, clamped, gagged, and ready to use.

I free the tag from her clamp and drop it onto the bed behind me. "Plugged, huh?" I ask her, my hand running down between her legs until I find the end of a dildo pressed tightly against the entrance to her cunt, the rest of it buried inside her. I move behind her and let my other hand roam down over her ass until my fingertips discover the base of another dildo, this one firmly up her arse.

My cock throbs at the thought of her like this for me and all the possibilities that I can do with her, so willing to be mine. I take a wrist in each hand and clip the restraints together in front of her, using them to lead her over to the bed. I sit and pull her over my lap on her front, her ass up in the air, her body across my knee. I put my left hand firmly between her shoulder blades and lean into her, keeping her immobilised with my hold.

With my right hand, I stroke careful circles over her upturned arse. I rub her skin, admiring the thong she has on to keep her dildos stuffed inside her, enjoying the feeling of her body over my upright dick. I know full well that she can feel me against her side, even through my jeans.

I pull on the end of the dildo in her pussy, teasing it in and out of her just a little bit, knowing it will drive her crazy and that she will need more. After just a few strokes, she starts to squirm against my hand, wriggling on my lap. The friction she's generating against my cock is too much, and I need to put a stop to it before she takes me too far. I raise my hand and smack it down hard on her backside.

Her skin heats at the contact. Her movement ceases, and she lies on my lap, waiting for what happens next. I lift my hand again and bring it down hard on her ass. I know it's moving the dildos she's got herself plugged with. I know it's intensifying the feeling they're generating within her, but she's been a bad girl to tease me like this, looking like she does when she dresses this way. She needs to learn her lesson. I keep letting my hand connect mercilessly with her buttocks until she's starting to moan against the gag and her ass cheeks are a fiery red.

If she's moaning, she's not getting a true taste of the lesson I'm trying to give her, so I decide to give her a taste of something else instead. I slide her from my lap to the floor in front of me.

"Give me your hands," I demand. She settles on her knees and presents her wrists to me. I unclip her wrists and pull her hands behind her back. The clasps click, and her arms are secured behind her.

Her chest rises and falls in rapid movements, making my dick lurch against my underwear and jeans. She really is the hottest woman I've ever known. There isn't a part of her that I don't find sexy, and knowing what I'm about to do to her, with her so willing and wanting, is driving me fucking crazy.

I stand before her; I undo the fly on my jeans and drop them to my knees. Her eyes follow my hands as they come back to my briefs. I rub the palm of my hand against my aching cock, knowing that watching me stroke myself gets her wet.

I tug my underwear to the same level as my jeans and grab my cock firmly in my hand, tugging along my length. Fuck, it feels so good, but not as good as it's going to feel when I do what I'm about to do.

"Like what you see, do you?" I ask, and she nods at me once. I smile and let my cock drop, sticking straight out, pointing at her. I let it rub across her lips, and her tongue snakes out around the gag, needing something more, wanting to take me in. I pull the strap at the side of her mouth, and the ball pops free. She licks her lips, her eyes on my dick, and she opens up, ready for me to slide into her wet mouth.

I close my eyes at the sheer fucking bliss that washes over me when I feel her enclose around me. My fist naturally balls in her hair, and I push that little bit deeper.

"Fuck!" I hiss when her tongue laps over the underside of my cock. "Oh, fuck. You're such a good girl for me."

It would be so easy to give into the temptation of using her mouth to bring me to the climax I'm already so desperately in need of reaching. It's just her; everything about her turns me on, but when she presents herself to me like this, it's doubly so. It's taking all of my reserve to not fuck her mouth roughly. I don't want to come until I'm buried deep inside her delicious, tight cunt.

That thought proves too much, and I pull myself from between her sweet lips. I grab the ball of the gag and push it back into her mouth, fixing the straps to hold it in place.

"Get up," I demand. She eases herself from the floor in front of me with relative ease, considering her hands were still behind her back. "Bend," I order again, putting a hand on her arm to direct her to the bed.

Once her knees hit the bed, she lets me guide her body to the mattress. Standing behind her for a split second, I admire the sight of her with her ass in the air and her face in the sheets. Stroking my aching dick, I step forward, sliding my finger into her knickers and pulling them aside, revealing the end of the dildo buried in her pussy.

Taking a hold of the toy plugging her, I unsheathe it from her cunt. It glistens with her juices, and unable to resist, I pull it to my lips and lick the length of it.

"Fuck, you taste so good," I tell her, savouring her taste. A frenzy starts in me, and I just can't resist anymore. In one movement, I slide my cock deep into her, feeling the extra tightness caused by her filled asshole.

She's so soaked that I'm able to sink balls deep inside her in just one movement.

"Oh, fuck," I groan when my cock is completely enshrouded in her warmth. My hands grip her hips, and driven by a deep need, I begin a rhythm of thrusts which pull me almost completely free of her before driving hard back inside.

Moaning vibrates through the bed, and I pick up the pace of my thrusts. I've allowed myself to get too worked up and now I need the release. I can't control the need to fuck her; I buck my hips against her as my fingers dig firmly into her skin.

"I'm going to come inside you," I warn her. "I'm going to fill you. I need to know that you're full of my cum."

My climax roars through me the second her pussy tightens around my cock as she is engulfed in her own orgasm. I use it to drive deep into her one last time.

I savour the pulses of her pussy as they milk the last of my cum from my cock before pulling out of her and collapsing on the bed beside her. I unclip her hands and pull her in against me. She pulls the gag from her mouth and moulds her body into my side.

"Don't remove anything," I whisper against the top of her head. "I'm not finished with you yet."

A contented sigh blows across my chest, and I hold her tight and nod off until I'm ready for round two.

Chapter Five

My heart is pounding in my chest as we walk into the hotel room. We had been talking about it for months now, and finally, we found someone we wanted to help us out. He's a nice guy, funny with a touch of cheeky, which put me completely at ease with him. He's into the same field of work as you, so you and he have been talking shop and getting on like a house on fire. Of course, this time it's going to be different.

Richie leads me towards the bed, leaving you behind to watch. He yanks me tight against him, his hands on my neck, and pulls me hard against him, his mouth enveloping mine, his tongue almost instantly probing my mouth. He presses hard against me in the kind of kiss that makes me feel like he just can't get enough of me or get me close enough. It's loaded with that raw, 'got to have you' sensation. I find it invigorating. Especially knowing you're there watching it all happen.

You move towards us and mould your body against my back, and your hands find my hips. Your length presses at my arse; you're already hard and all he's done is kiss me.

Your lips find my neck, and he stops kissing me to watch what you're doing. When you lift your head to look at him, I see that flash in both your eyes. You both lean over my shoulder, utilising the fact that I'm shorter than you to move in and kiss each other. I watch, wedged between you, feeling you both grind against me as you let your tongues explore each other's mouths. My pussy is already soaked from finding myself smack in the middle of the sexiest thing I've ever seen. One delicious hot red-blooded male getting off on another.

I try to slip away from between the two of you, intent on getting a better view of what's happening, and instead, you grab me around the waist and pull me back against you both. Richie's hands go for mine, and he guides me over his cock and yours, pressing my palm against you both, telling me what he wants from me while never breaking his physical connection to you.

You both roll your hips against my hand as I press hard against you. I feel how hard you both are, how turned on and needy you're both getting as you push yourselves against my hands. I drop my hand from his cock, and I move to free yours, undoing your jeans and moving them just enough to let your cock free. I then do the same with Richie's. When you're both exposed to me, I can't help but bend between you and lick along the heads of both your dicks.

You and Richie gasp, breaking your kiss and staring down at me and what I'm doing. I gaze up at you both, taking one of you into my wet mouth before swapping sides and taking in the other. I alternate between your delicious cocks, lapping at each of you, sucking on you both. I look up at you and see you watching me while I suck on Richie, and I know that look only too well.

"Do you want to taste him?" I ask you before I sink my mouth back over you again. You moan as I do.

"Oh, fuck, yes," you breathe, and Richie smirks at your answer.

Richie takes a step back from us. He pulls his t-shirt over his head, revealing his lean torso and speckling of manly body hair. His jeans and boxers disappear too, and he stands there in all his full glory. I glance at you as your eyes feast on him all over. I smirk and catch your eye.

"I think you're just a little bit overdressed now, my love," I tease, and you don't hesitate in taking off your t-shirt and jeans and standing in front of us both naked.

My eyes feast on you, naked, broad-shouldered, and all that delicious chest hair I can't keep my hands off.

"Get on your knees," I demand.

Your hands instinctively cover your cock while you sink to the floor. I get up and move behind Richie, pushing him closer to you until he's standing right in front of you. I reach around him and wrap my hand around his cock, pumping him a few times, keeping my eyes fixed on you as I do.

"Open your mouth," I tell you.

You do, and I push him one step closer to you, his cock just in front of your face. I move to his side, reach out, grab you by the back of the head, and shove your face and waiting open mouth over Richie's cock. I set the speed and movement of you both together, him thrusting and you pushing your mouth against him to take him even deeper. Once your hands reach for his thighs to pull him against you, I let you both go and bend to whisper loudly in your ear.

"You love sucking a real cock, don't you, my little queer?" I ask.

You moan, and Richie's eyes roll back in his head at the

sensation of you murmuring around his cock. I run my hands over his body, grazing over his nipples as I do. Once utterly satisfied with the floor show, I step back and rest myself on the bottom of the bed to watch.

Richie's hand takes hold of the back of your head. He's intently watching his cock slip in and out past your lips. You're looking up at him, focused on taking all of him into your mouth. I'm watching, lying back on the bed, running my hands over my clothing. I'm so utterly turned on by what I'm seeing. My hot alpha man with this younger guy, doing things that, until now, he has only dreamed of doing.

My hand grazes the inside of my thigh as I watch, transfixed at the glorious sight of you being face fucked for the first time by another man. I slip my hand into the waistband of my lacy knickers, and I spread myself wide, needing to take care of myself while you too skilfully take care of Richie. One stroke of my fingers over my cunt confirms what I already knew; I am utterly soaked, turned on so much by what I'm experiencing right now.

Richie watches me run my fingertips over my clit, soft moans falling from my lips. He watches me watching him, and I know it's only adding to his arousal. His grip tightens at the back of your neck, his breathing a little erratic as he watches me playing with myself. I gaze at you as you look at what I'm doing too. I hear your moan, and when I do, Richie's head drops back and he's lodging himself at the back of your throat. He groans, and I watch you gag. My own climax rises in my groin. I know he's pumping your mouth full of his hot cum, and you're loving every minute while I play with my pussy for you both.

He steps back and lets his semi-erect cock slide from between your lips, and your eyes are still focused on me as he sits down in the armchair in the corner of the room. I know the look on your face, and I watch as you rise from the floor and move towards me. I move back on the bed, knowing you're coming for me like I'm prey. You follow me over the bed, lining yourself up between my legs. Your body covers mine and you lean down and kiss me, hard and hungry. The taste of Richie's cum is still all over your tongue and you roll it over mine.

You sit up on your knees and look down at me. You spread my legs wider and tug the crotch of my knickers to the side, waiting for nothing as you push your cock inside me in one stroke.

"Did you enjoy sucking a real cock?" I ask with a smile.

"I did," you tell me.

I gasp as you press your cock into the deepest parts of me with the next thrust. "And did you enjoy drinking his cum, my little slut?"

"Oh, fuck, yes," you say with a roll of your hips.

You pick up the pace and mix things up with a roll of your hips and hard, deep thrusts on every stroke. You tease me to orgasm again and again, while Richie watches. I look at him by the time I'm coming back down from my third climax and notice he's hard again, stroking his cock as he surveys the show we're putting on.

The thrill of having a witness to our fucking washes over me, and I can't help but come even harder the next time. He stands when I do, moving over towards the bed, his cock in his hand, jerking his length as he disappears behind you. I hear him flick the lid on a bottle of lube as he reappears in my line of sight, directly behind you.

"Wait," he tells you, with a hand on your back as you have yourself deep in my wet pussy. He manoeuvres behind you, and your cock twitches inside me when the head of his cock rubs against your asshole. This is what you've been waiting for, to have your ass fucked hard by a real cock that can leave a hot load deep inside you.

I wrap my legs around your thighs and pull your legs apart slightly, holding you tight against me, yet giving Richie more access to your slutty little arsehole. I know the second he has penetrated you because your whole body tenses for an instant and then relaxes. I wait, letting Richie work his way deep into your ass before he starts thrusting against you. You both start to move, setting a rhythm that suits you. You pull back from my pussy and push back on him, then sink back into me hard, as I'm pounded with the force of two driving forward.

You set a harsh pace with each other. Driving hard against each other and taking me along for the ride with you. I climax over and over as Richie fucks your ass hard, and you fuck my cunt as deeply as you can.

"Oh, God! Tell him where you want his cum, you fucking slut," I demand of you.

You moan and grind harder against me.

"Tell me," Richie commands.

"Fuck!" you pant. "Up my ass. Ohh, fuck! Come up my gay ass." You sigh on a moan.

Richie's pace picks up again, his hands grabbing your hips. "I'm going to fill your arse, you little bitch. Fucking take it," he growls. His words make me climax, and with him unloading his cum in your ass and me clenching your cock and soaking it more, you let go, roaring as your whole body jerks, and you flood my pussy with your cum.

He slips from your ass and moves off the bed, positioning himself near your face. "Suck it," he tells you, and you run your mouth hungrily over his cock. Once satisfied with your clean-up job, he encourages you to move back and out of my cunt. He dips his head as you do, and you hiss as he licks my juices from your cock.

Richie drops himself down on the bed beside me. You drop on the other side, and the three of us lie there, caressing each other lovingly as we all come down from our powerful climaxes. Each of you rests a head on one of my breasts, and I kiss the top of your heads.

"What a perfect little pair of filthy little queers you are," I tease. I can't wait to see what the rest of the evening holds for us all.

Chapter Six

When she finally gets home, I need to be inside her immediately. Hell, I have since before she left for work this morning, when I pulled her knickers aside, slid into her, and pumped her full of my cum.

I wanted her to smell me on her pussy all day. I wanted her to have a constant reminder of where I had been and what I had done. I needed to have her thinking of me as much as I'd be thinking of her at work, in that dress she knows drives me crazy. She's mine, and I like to keep reminding her of it. I like to keep marking my territory, claiming her with cum.

I move towards her after she closes the door. She smiles at me, and I wrap my arms around her and hug her tight against me, needing her close. I lean in and place my lips against her neck, softly at first. Then, I can't help myself. She presses against me, and I draw her skin harder against my mouth with a suck. I know it's going to mark her, but I really can't resist it.

Her head falls back, and a moan escapes her lips. It's all I need to tip me over. I grab at the skirt of her dress, tugging it up enough for me to dip my hand below the hem. My hand runs along her stocking-covered thigh as my mouth moves back to hers before I find the edge of her lacy knickers and waste no time in plunging a finger deep into her cunt. She's so fucking wet, as I knew she would be.

"That's my good girl," I purr against her lips, and I work a second finger deep into her, starting a steady thrust with my hand. "Always so fucking wet and ready for me, aren't you?"

A moan is her only reply, and the slight blush on her cheeks tells me how right I am, and how much she's enjoying being called a good girl. I slip a third finger against the other two, and I let my thumb roll over her clit as she grinds against the stroke of my hand. She's getting so close to coming for me already.

"Mmm, that's my good girl. You want to come, don't you?" I ask.

"Oh, fuck, yes!" she tells me, her breathing rapid and her heart pounding.

There are two ways I can play this. I can either give her the orgasm she so desperately craves already, or I could pull my hand out of her pussy now and lick my fingers as I walk away. But she gives me that look, the one I know too well, and I know it will only end one way. With her quaking around my fingers as her juices coat my hand.

I rub her clit a little bit faster, with a touch more pressure, as I push my fingers as deeply as she can take them. I look at her, catching her gaze, making sure she can't look away, and I say what she needs to hear. "Come for me."

She coats my fingers and hand in the seconds after I've said it. I'm so fucking hard for her; I press myself against her as she cries out against me. "Such a good fucking girl." I smile and press my lips on hers, swallowing her moans of satisfaction.

When I pull my fingers from inside her, she shakes against me at their loss, but I already have other ideas of what will happen next. I step back from her, and one by one, I take each of my fingers and suck her from them. I fucking love how she tastes, and I will definitely be feasting on her afterwards. For now, I have a cock that's painfully rubbing against my underwear and jeans, and I know just the place for it.

I push her shoulder, and she needs no further encouragement or instruction. Her knees bend and she sinks to the floor, looking up at me expectantly. I undo my jeans and gaze at her.

"You know what I want," I tell her. And she does.

She takes my jeans and pulls them to my knees, her hands running over my skin, caressing my thighs as she returns to my briefs. She stares up with eyes filled with lust and satisfaction and runs her palm firmly over my swollen length.

"Fuck," I groan, putting both hands on the wall behind her, far above her head, bracing myself for what she's about to do.

Her hands rub again over my cock, and I glare at her, silently telling her not to try that again; I won't be able to take her teasing me. She knows me well enough to pull my briefs down to meet my jeans and let my dick spring out in front of her. She looks at it, licking her lips like it's a meal she's been dying for all day, then closes her eyes as she takes me into her warm, wet mouth.

Fuck, she really is too much. I rest my head on the wall in front of me, my eyes closed, and just enjoy every sensation that's washing over me. The feel of her tongue on the bottom side of my dick. The wetness of her saliva as she spreads it over me. The strength of her suck when she pulls me deep into her sweet little mouth.

Just as I lose myself in that feeling, her hands arrive on my outer thighs. She shifts below me, getting comfortable as she grabs my ass and pulls me deeper into her. The head of my cock hits her gag reflex. I open my eyes and look down to find her looking up at me. Her eyes start to water as she fights the natural urge to expel what's in her throat.

I'm about to pull back from her just a little when I feel her finger against my asshole. "Oh, fuck. That's my good girl," I tell her, pulling back out of her mouth just enough to let her get her breath before she pushes her finger partway into my ass. I can't help but thrust forward. Every movement I make in her mouth, she makes with her finger in my ass, and I know if she keeps that up, she'll be swallowing the load I've been saving for her all day. But that's not where I want it to go. I enjoy the feeling of her finger getting deeper and deeper up my arse as I push my cock repeatedly against the back of her throat.

She looks sexy as hell when I look down on her and see her eyes wet from taking me deep and encouraging me to fuck her gorgeous face. The need to be buried deep in her pussy is more than I can bear when I look at how amazing my dick looks sinking into her sweet mouth.

I force myself to pull my cock from between her lips, and she lets me, her finger slipping from my ass. She repeats my actions and slides her finger between her lips and licks it, tasting me. I heave my jeans and briefs from half-mast, then grab her wrists and pull her to her feet, guiding her through the house until we reach the bedroom.

"Hands and knees," I demand as she looks over her shoulder at me. She lifts the hem of her dress so she doesn't kneel on it and crawls onto the bed, kneeling just as I asked her to. This time the jeans and briefs come off, along with my t-shirt, soon standing behind her completely naked. Joining her on the bed from behind, letting my hands stroke her thighs up under her dress lifting it completely, leaving her sexy ass exposed to me.

I have teased myself as well as her, and I can't wait any longer than I need to. As much as I love the sight of her naked and spread for me, that would just take too fucking long. I find the crotch of her knickers, pull them to the side, and guide my cock into her soaked slit.

I slide into her in one stroke, balls deep in her tight little pussy. I know by how she clenches me when I'm as deep as I can be that she's felt the stretch she tells me is so delicious. I pull back, watching my cock move out of her, slick with her juices before I delight in the sight of it sliding all the way back inside her. Fuck, I could watch that for hours. There is no sight more gorgeous to me than that of her beautiful pussy taking all of my bare cock, just like it was made for that very activity. However, hours of this would have my balls blue enough to drop off.

I push against her and she pushes back on me; looking to feel me just that little bit deeper. My girl is always so greedy for what I have to give her. I hold on to her hips as I pump into her hard and fast. She clamps down around me, and I know another orgasm is about to rip through her. She cries out and clenches down on my cock so hard I stop moving, buried as deep as I can be, and enjoy the waves of climax as they flood around my dick and grip me hard.

When I feel her relax, I pick up the pace, thrusting deep and hard, knowing she'll come again pretty soon. I need her to; every time she does it pushes me closer to my own peak. I thrust and thrust, stopping only as a few more of her orgasms grip my cock, until she pushes me past the point where I could stop. I feel it starting in my balls, and I know I'm going to fill her with cum.

"Oh, fuck. I'm going to come. Where do you want it?" I pant.

A groan rumbles through her and she pushes back on me again. "Oh, God. You'd better flood my cunt. I need it... oh, God!" she begs. "Give me your cum!"

Her pussy tightens again as she speaks those words, but I can't think or hold back any longer. I slam deep inside her as she says it and unload into her, flooding her just as she asked me to.

I pull her onto her side with me, still hard enough to remain buried deep inside her as I do. I wrap my arms around her as we both come back down to earth from the heavens above. I hold her tight against me, utterly content that her sweet little cunt is full of me and my cum. I will savour its taste and smell it up close when she's sitting on my face, but for now, I'm very pleased to leave some of myself deep inside her.

Owned

'A truly submissive woman is to be treasured, cherished and protected for it is only she who can give a man the gift of dominance.'

    - Anne Desclos

Prologue

I had never really seen myself as a submissive. Quite the opposite, in fact. I was always dominating situations I was in, including sexually. Even if I was the subservient in the relationship, I still schemed, pushed, and 'topped from the bottom.' But my world fell apart when my partner took off with his secretary. I decided it was time for some changes. Time for some fun. That's how I met Owen.

I've known Owen for about five years now. I met him when I went to play some pool at the local university's bar with a few of the students I worked with. Owen was in his twenties, from Wales, and a student at the same university. I was in my early thirties. We flirted, we teased each other. We even had a very short period of dating, but in the end, we became best friends. I never would have dreamed it would turn out to be a lot more than that. My hot Welsh friend had a secret I didn't find out for a few years. He was a dominant: a Dom, a Master, a Sir.

At first, I thought nothing of it. I knew I wasn't like that, but the more Owen gave me glimpses into his world, the more intrigued I became. He led me down the path to submission, like the white rabbit leading Alice into Wonderland. Now, I'm hooked. I'm addicted to the pleasure only he can generate in me. I am his.

I am HIS.

Chapter One

I remember the first time with Owen taking control like it was yesterday. I was no stranger to Owen, his house, or even his body. We had fooled around countless times before, but this time would be the first I let him exclusively take the lead. We had discussed what I would like to try and the things he liked. He said he would work out the details and everything else that brought me here, standing on his doorstep, following his instructions.

I'm wearing the lacy sheer underwear and jersey maxi dress he insisted on. The stockings and the knee-high high-heeled boots are my own addition to the outfit. I take a deep breath, trying to calm down my accelerating heart, and I knock on the door.

Owen stands there in a t-shirt, jeans, and his feet bare, his eyes glistening as he looks me over before standing aside to let me in. When I step inside, he steps in behind me.

"Can I take your jacket?" he breathes at my neck while already pulling the denim from my shoulders. This simple act seems heightened by the situation. My skin tingles everywhere the denim brushes.

"Turn," he commands. "Let me look at you." I turn around on the spot for him, allowing him to take me in, letting his eyes roam over me. In a split second, he has me pinned against the wall in the hallway. His mouth descends over mine, and his tongue finds its way to mine, licking and caressing it as they roll over one another. His kiss is hungry and possessive, and his hands roam from my face down my body to my hips. He presses me harder against the wall before his hands settle around my wrists, trapping them.

He breaks our kiss and pulls my arms up over my head, pinning my hands to the wall above me. He shifts his hands so he's able to circle both my wrists in one hand, leaving the other free to caress over my body. It goes straight back to my hip, and he starts to crumple the material of my dress up, pulling the hem higher and higher until he can step back and look freely at what's underneath. When his eyes fall on my stockings and boots, they darken, and he holds my gaze with an unforgiving stare. Again, his lips collide with mine, more possessive than before, and his free hand goes to my lacy knickers.

He pulls back the waistband and slips his hand inside them until he's where he wants to be, directly between my legs. He uses his knee to force my legs apart. When he does, he pushes my legs out further, forcing me to move my feet, my legs wider, and his access is uninhibited. He wastes no time; his fingers move between my slick folds and he's inside me. I gasp against his mouth as his fingers drive deep, and he starts to fingerfuck me against his hallway wall.

The second my hips instinctively grind back against his touch, he breaks our kiss, pulls his fingers from me, and makes a great show of licking his slickened fingers, savouring the wetness like he's licking chocolate from his digits. He uses the hand that holds my wrists to pull me along behind him into his joined living room-dining room. He drags me in front of him, facing his dining room table. He pushes me forward, just a fraction, so my palms are resting on the tabletop. His knee again goes between my legs, and this time he forces me to spread my legs wider. My mind is racing with thoughts of what is to come. I bite my lower lip in expectation.

Owen's hands grab at my dress again, pulling it up, stopping only when it's bunched at my waist and my ass is exposed. He presses himself against my ass, and I feel the hard length of him through his jeans. He holds me firmly at the back of the neck and pushes my face to the cool surface of the tabletop. "You will *not* move," he commands, and my cheeks heat as I'm told what to do.

Owen's hand connects with my backside with a satisfying crack, and the initial sting settles into a burn that simmers through my ass, pussy, and clit.

"I didn't tell you to wear boots and stockings," he says as he smacks my arse again.

"No, Sir," I stammer, surprised at just how much being spanked is turning me on.

"I like them, so just this once I'll let you off with it. But don't think you'll be getting away with it ever again. Understood?" he asks as he continues to rain smacks on my buttocks.

"Yes, Sir."

Owen's hand strokes over my ass, and I hear his zipper being lowered. Before I know what's happening, he has yanked my underwear to the side and buried his cock deep into my pussy. He grabs my hips harshly and starts to pound into me without ceremony. "I don't like it when you don't do what you're told, girl," he warns as he thrusts hard and deep into my soaked sex.

There's something primal in the way he's taking me. Suddenly, I can see the appeal of submission all the more. I'm certainly enjoying the harsh fucking I'm getting, but I'm also feeling the need to atone for my indiscretion, to be back in his good favour, to allow him anything he needs for me to achieve that.

His fucking becomes more fervoured, and suddenly I realise this isn't about being fucked; this is about him taking what he wants, rushing to the finish line. He's using me as a means to an end, reinforcing my place within this little game of ours. My orgasm is only just starting to build and his is already about to wash over him. His fingers dig into my hips as he roars out in climax behind me, thrusting in as completely as he can before he spills his load deep inside me.

As soon as he's done, he withdraws from me and fixes my underwear back across my pussy. Sheer frustration washes over me. I'm so incredibly turned on, and I want nothing more than to climax, but I'm denied. Owen drops my dress back down over my backside.

He helps me get back up from the table and commands me to kneel in front of him. He holds his wet cock out in front of me. "Taste it," he commands. "Clean me up and see what you taste like."

I close my eyes and open my mouth, my lips surrounding his semi-erect dick. My taste buds are flooded with the flavour of my juices mixed with his, and I can't help but lick him greedily. I wouldn't have thought I would like to taste myself, but the frustration and the feeling of just how wet my pussy is against my knickers just adds to the sensation.

When he's satisfied with the job I've done and well on the way to being hard again, he leads me back over to the sofa and tells me to sit down. With every move, I can feel the juices leaking from my pussy and covering my underwear.

I see the slight grin pulling at the edges of his mouth. "Feeling good?" he asks me, clearly knowing too well how this feels. I shift in my seat and his grin spreads.

"Yes, Sir," I sigh.

"Have we learned a lesson now, girl? You're mine to use as I see fit. Even if that's using you to get myself off. You getting off is not a concern," he reminds me. Suddenly, I begin to wish I hadn't even mentioned the notion of orgasm denial. I'm beginning to see just how much knowledge he has on that very subject. I'm now sure of two very important things. One, Owen is not going to let me come today, and two, when he finally does allow it, I'm going to explode like a damn rocket.

For the rest of the day, Owen repeats the same process. He pulls my knickers to the side, fucks me hard, and spills into me. Then he straightens my underwear back up and carries on with the rest of my submissive experimentation. By the end of the day, my pussy is saturated with his cum and mine, and my lacy underwear is just as bad.

When the last 'game' of the day arrives, Owen strips me naked and ties me down over his dining room table. He tells me he's going to bury his cock in my ass, and that he's been looking forward to it all day. He tells me to open my mouth. When I do, my drenched knickers are shoved in as a gag and a tie tightened around my mouth to hold them in place.

When Owen pushes his cock into my ass, every frustrated nerve in my body is set on fire. As he fucks me slow and deep, a tsunami of pleasure takes hold of me. When I finally climax, it's so powerful that I'm sure all of the bones in my body have been removed and speech will never be possible again. That was the first time I ever knew what it was like to be someone else's. The first time I knew I would do anything to keep Owen happy if this was my reward. The first time he became *my* Master O.

Chapter Two

Sir was very vague in his instructions. He told me what to wear, where to be, but very little else. That's why I'm here in a deserted park at dusk, on a warm summer's evening, wearing a jersey maxi dress and white cotton underwear.

I do as I am told. I take a stroll around the outer path of the park, enjoying the last sunshine of the day. The cool breeze makes me feel aware of my skin. Anticipation of what is due to come has me wet, and the breeze stiffens my nipples and causes goose bumps to form on my skin.

I hear a twig snap behind me, and I turn to see if anyone is there. Finding no one, I turn again and continue on my walk. The sun finally starts to disappear, and shadows are forming around the picnic area as I pass. I feel like I'm being followed. Before I have the chance to turn and look, a hand is over my mouth and an arm is around my waist, lifting me off my feet and pulling me tight against the body behind me.

I feel his breath on my ear, and he whispers, "You need to keep quiet. If you don't, I know where you live. Understand, *little pet?*"

I swallow hard. It wasn't until the comment of 'little pet' that I realised what was happening, but the person behind me isn't Master O. At least, that's what I think.

I'm hoisted towards the shadows at the picnic area and pushed against a table in front of me, my 'attacker' behind me.

The hand at my waist moves to my hips and starts to pull up my dress. When he pulls me against him tightly, I can feel his hard cock against the small of my back. Cold metal slides against my hip and one side of my knickers gives way. I tense in his grip and attempt to scream, my heart racing at the thought of him brandishing a knife.

"Yeah, you feel that, don't you? You're going to do as you're told now, aren't you?" he breathes against my ear. I can hear the smile in his voice, and I shiver.

I feel him manoeuvring himself; the other side of my dress is also gathered up. The cold of the knife sends goose bumps over my skin as he cuts through the other side of my knickers and pulls them off in one move.

"Now, my little one, you're not going to move, are you?" he asks rhetorically as he grinds his hips against my back, brings his knife-holding hand to my mouth, and lifts the other just long enough to shove my balled up knickers into my mouth as a gag. He takes my hands, pulling them behind my back, and quickly restrains them there. I'm standing there in the middle of a darkened, deserted park, gagged, restrained, and with no panties on.

He pushes my legs further apart with his knees, his hands reaching up my body, cupping my breasts before groping and squeezing them roughly. He grabs at the top of my dress and yanks it down, exposing my white cotton bra. He roughly grabs at my breasts again, pulling on my nipples through the cotton before grabbing at the cups and pulling those down too, letting my breasts spill out over the top. He paws at me roughly, his hands kneading painfully into my flesh. I should cry out, but instead, I moan into the makeshift gag in my mouth.

"You're enjoying it aren't you, you little whore?" he chides me, breathing hotly across my ear. His unforgiving hands pull at my nipples, twisting them painfully. "You're going to take just what I give you, bitch, and you're going to like it, because all little sluts like a man to give them it hard, don't they?"

I whimper into the gag as he releases my hands and bends me over the table. My dress is once again lifted, this time exposing me to the cool evening air, my sex and ass now bare for anyone who cares to see. He kicks my feet, widening my stance again as he puts his hands on my bound wrists behind my back and pushes down on them. I'm flat against the bench, the still sun-warmed wood rough against my tender tits. He runs his hand along my slick pussy and plucks at my clit with his fingers, giving it a sharp squeeze. "Remember who you're dealing with, slut," he reminds me as I cry out into the knickers in my mouth.

His hand connects with my bare ass in a brutal wallop. The jolt carries me forward a little, rubbing my nipples against the jagged grain of the table. "Just for now, this is mine," he hisses at me in the encroaching darkness. "My ass, my pussy, my little whore, and I will do whatever the fuck I want with her." His fingers again run through my slick cunt, and he chuckles to himself. "All turned on and wet because she's getting fucked in the park for the world to see what a whore she is. Seems like I picked the right little pet," he mocks and thrusts two fingers deep into my soaked sex and begins fucking me roughly with them.

He withdraws them just as abruptly as he inserted

them, and again, his hand cracks down hard on my ass. The skin on my buttocks stings, sizzling right through to my clit. I shouldn't be enjoying this, but I am, and what's worse is he knows it. I hear his zipper, and a second later, I feel his skin against mine as he plunges his cock inside me. I cry out against his harsh penetration and his rough handling of me, but the gag in my mouth makes my sounds nothing more than a muffled moan.

"What's that, slut? You like my dick deep in your greedy little snatch? Mmmm, I think I agree with you on that one!" He gloats as he grabs my hair and pulls me upright against him. He rams into me with great force while he holds onto my breasts to keep us together. The harder he thrusts, the more his fingers dig into my flesh, grabbing me, bruising me as he squeezes my tits tightly.

He thrusts up hard and stops, pausing with me impaled on his cock, while he takes the time to cup my breasts more gently, pulling harshly on the nipples and twisting them cruelly. "Bet you're getting off on this, aren't you?" he whispers in my ear before biting my earlobe. I know that if this was real, I would be terrified, but he's right. I'm beyond turned on right now. I'm aching to have him thrust into me just a little bit harder, to pull on my breasts and nipples, and to have my screams of pleasure echo around this park. But I'm not the one in control here, and he's making that abundantly clear.

He moves his hands from my breasts to around my neck, holding me tight against him by the throat, my head tilted back as he bites into my shoulder. I cry into the knickers in my mouth, relishing the delicious pain he's inflicting on me. I try and move my hips to get the sweet climax I'm craving so badly, but he holds himself firm and keeps me pinned against him, forced to do the same.

"This isn't for you, dear," he sneers and pushes me forward. I lose my balance, and without my hands to save myself, I come down hard on the table, chest first, the rough wood biting into my skin. The harshness of the landing I receive is only intensified by the absence of his dick in my pussy. Before I know it, his hand is connecting with my ass cheeks again, over and over, reinforcing the point that this is not about my pleasure or me in anyway. This is a lesson in service, in taking what I am getting, regardless of what I want. Suddenly, Master O's keenness over my little rape fantasy is so very clear. I wanted the thrill of it, and he's teaching me that it's not about me. He's the one with the control; he's the one who understands my needs better than I do, that the submission is what helps me best deal with the situation.

When he's done smacking my ass, he rubs his hands over my scorched skin. I groan against my gag, on edge, needing to come, and not knowing what his next move will be. It isn't long before I find out. Fingers back in my wet pussy, rubbing everywhere, spreading my slickness around towards my ass. I tense; he couldn't possibly mean to fuck me in the ass like this, could he? His thumb teases over my asshole, and it's not long before I get my answer. The head of his cock pushes hard against my ass, demanding entrance.

He's not as lubricated as I'm used to, and there's a sharp sting as he pushes past the ring of muscle and forces his way into my ass until he is firmly embedded deep inside. I want him to take a minute to let me adjust, but I know it's not likely to happen when he starts to thrust into me, pushing ever deeper. When his balls press against my pussy, I know that's as far as he can physically go. I can't lie; it's not comfortable. It's not the vision I had in my mind when I told Sir about my darkest fantasies, but I also know I'm not so restrained that I can't just spit out my panties and scream my safe word if I want to. The thing is, I don't want to. I bite a little harder on the gag in my mouth when he withdraws almost completely to slam back into me. Soon enough, I'm moaning into my gag again, seeking that sweet sensation overload that only orgasm can bring me. But I can feel the cock buried in my ass begin to pulse. I know no matter what I want to achieve, he's about to get what he wants, and that's all that should matter to me. I hear him roar behind me, I feel him explode deep in my ass, and I wince at how hard he's gripping my hips to make sure he comes as deeply in my arse as he can.

My frustration is almost blinding, and I'm only vaguely aware of him pulling out of me. The next thing I know, my wrists are free, and as I slowly lift myself off the table on aching arms, he is nowhere to be seen. I pull my knickers from my mouth and look at the cut sides. I let the skirt of my dress fall back to my ankles, as it was when I first walked into the park. I adjust my bra and the top of my dress, recovering my breasts, making sure that if I bump into anyone, they would not be aware of what happened to me.

For a split second, I think about relieving my frustrations right there in the park. It wouldn't take long. I could hop on the tabletop, part my legs, let my dress ride up, and give myself the orgasm I so desperately crave. But that notion passes, replaced with slight guilt and a need to follow the rules of the scene that had unravelled before me. No matter what happens, I will not come by my own means.

Once steady on my feet and sure I'm at least outwardly suitable to finish my walk and get out of the park, I start towards the exit. As I pass by the gate, I see Master O's car and him inside. He beckons me over, and I approach.

"Get in," he commands. I open the door and slip into the seat beside him. "Nice walk?" He grins.

I nod, unable to put into words how I truly feel about the situation. Frustrated doesn't seem to cut it.

"Here..." he says, holding out a handful of items for me to take from him. "Put these in the glove box."

I look down, and in my hands, I see a knife and some cable ties.

"It was you?" I ask.

"Always, my sweet. You didn't think I would leave such an event to someone else, did you?"

I think about it for a second. Knowing how Sir handles things, honestly? No, I couldn't see him letting someone else experience with me what I just had.

"No, Sir," I agree with a sigh.

He glances over at me and grins as he starts the car. "Let's get you home. I think there's something I need to take care of for you." He smiles and leans over to my side of the car, placing his lips against mine, sliding his hand up under my dress and between my legs. He circles my clit, and the pent-up frustration has me exploding over his hand in mere moments.

He removes his fingers from under my dress, licking them as if they were the most delicious things he had ever tasted. "That will do, for now. At least until we get back to mine." He smirks, turns on the car headlights, and drives off into the twilight.

Chapter Three

Sir walks into the room with a bag in his hand and orders me to strip. I follow his commands quickly. I drop my jeans and panties to the floor before setting them on the armchair carefully, followed by my t-shirt and bra soon after. I stand there in the middle of Master O's living room completely naked, my head bowed, my chest out, and my arms flat by my sides. I stand with my feet shoulder-width apart, so my sex is always slightly exposed.

Sir opens his bag and produces his first gift for me. It's a collar, very similar to one a dog would have. He fastens a leash made from a metal chain and a leather wrist strap to the collar. Master O pulls on the leash, tugging me down, forcing me to move to my knees to prevent falling over. Once I'm on my knees, Master O tugs the leash again so I naturally fall forward onto all fours.

"Don't move," he commands, and I know I'll be remaining on my hands and knees for the rest of the session.

Sir returns to the bag again and produces two mitten-like gloves. It's not until he feeds my hand into one that I realise what they are. They are made from fur and leather and have been fashioned to look rather like paws.

Inside, they are designed to offer support to my wrists yet make my hands completely immobile and useless. He buckles each one tight. I know I wouldn't be able to get them off for myself, even if I wanted to.

Once my front paws have been secured firmly in place, Sir again returns to his bag. This time, he produces kneepads. He taps on my thigh, so I can lift my leg and allow him to fasten my kneepads in place. Once complete, I am left very comfortably on all fours.

Master O pulls on my leash, prompting me to turn with his tug as he manoeuvres me to a different position.

"You know what you are, don't you?" he asks.

I nod my head. "Yes, Sir," I reply.

"What are you?"

"Your dog, Sir."

"No." He laughs, "You're my bitch!"

I nod, accepting what is to come. "Yes, Sir."

Again, Master O dips into the bag he brought into the room. In his hand, he holds a strap with a strange piece of metal on it. It looks almost like a snaffle bit for a horse, but not quite. He tilts my head back and forces my mouth open with his thumb.

"Your tongue," he commands.

I stick my tongue out of my open mouth, and Sir slips the contraption over my tongue then pushes it all back into my mouth. The metal bracket naturally sits around the back of my bottom teeth and sandwiches my tongue between two further pieces, trapping it in such a way it's impossible to form any kind of words or speech. Instead, I can only groan or growl. Sir secures the device around my head tightly, and all speech is removed. I am purely his little dog. Indeed, I'm his bitch.

Sir returns to his bag once more and one final item is produced to complete my transformation. I face forward and stay completely still. I hear the little bottle in his hand flip open, and I wait to feel it. Cool gel tickles down between my buttocks to my asshole. Sir rubs the end of his last gift in the gel before pressing it against my arsehole firmly. I breathe deeply as he pushes against the tight muscles until suddenly, they give way. As a strange groan escapes my gagged mouth, my ass is filled with a fat plug. My ass tightens around the tapered part of the plug. Knowing it's now secure, I glance back over my shoulder, greeted by an extraordinary sight. Master O has given me a tail. It's long and looks like soft silicone, supple enough that every movement I make is translated into a wag of my tail by the soft rubber.

Sir rubs his hand over my back. "That's a good girl." He smiles. "Your name is now Ginger, and you're my little bitch. I expect you to be a good little dog. You will sit, stay, play fetch, go for walks, and if I need to, I will take you to the vet. Your food and water dishes are on the floor in the kitchen, and when you need the bathroom, you'd better scratch the door to be let out into the garden," he warns.

Heat creeps over my face at the humiliating thought of what he's just said.

"Now," he says, looking at his watch. "The vet should be here soon to check on my little bitch's health. Shall we play a game until then?" He grins.

A small sense of dread creeps over me. A vet? I don't get time to dwell on it any further, as Sir lifts a squeaky chew toy from his bag and squeezes it so it gets my attention.

He tosses it across the room, and I happily trot after it

on all fours before grabbing it with my limited mouth mobility and bringing it back to Master O. He pats my head and praises me. I can't help but feel a delighted warmth creep through me. I have pleased him, which in turn pleases me. Again, he squeezes my toy, making it squeak before throwing it and letting me trot after it again. Our game continues for a while, until the doorbell rings, and Sir lifts my leash and pulls me behind him as he goes to the door.

When he opens it, I see his friend, Thomas, standing there. Thomas shakes Sir's hand, glances at me, and says, "Is this the bitch you called me to the house about?"

Sir nods. "Thanks for doing a house call." He smiles and leads Thomas into the living room with me pulled along behind.

"Where do you want her?" Sir asks, and Thomas points to the dining room table.

"Up there should be good enough."

I'm pulled to the table, where Sir then lifts me and sets me on it, still on all fours.

Thomas pulls surgical gloves from his bag and puts them on. Then, out comes a stethoscope. He rubs the cold plate over my breasts before finally settling on the right position. He listens to my chest before nodding and putting it away again. He pulls my mouth open as much as he can around my strange gag and runs his gloved fingers over my trapped tongue.

A large syringe with no needle comes out of a box he has in his bag next.

"This will treat her for worms and fleas," he tells Sir before shoving the syringe to the back of my throat and emptying it. I recognise the taste instantly. This vet's 'medicine' is cum. "She'll need this regularly, Owen," Sir is told.

Thomas's hands rub over my whole body, as though he really is inspecting me. His hands cup my dangling breasts and squeeze hard before pulling on the stiff little peaks of my nipples. His hands run down my back and over my buttocks. He pushes on the plug, which is held firmly in my ass. Without ceremony, two gloved fingers are shoved inside me, causing me to whimper.

"There, girl," Sir coos while stroking my head. "What do you think?" he asks.

"Oh, she's definitely good breeding stock," Thomas confirms. Sir grins at me, and I'm suddenly dreading what's going to happen next.

"Have you thought about having her microchipped?" Thomas asks.

I flinch; he can't possibly be serious. I shift around on the tabletop, but Sir yanks my leash hard and tells me to stay. He looks again at Thomas. "If she's as good a breeding bitch as you think she is, I guess I'd better," he announces.

I'm starting to panic. Thomas reaches into his bag again and pulls out a sealed pack, with a rather mean-looking syringe and a tag reader. I shift nervously on the tabletop.

"Hold her still!" Thomas demands.

Sir wraps his arm around my waist, facing towards my backside, and uses a tight bear grip to hold me still. Thomas smacks my right buttock before rubbing over it with a cold antiseptic wipe. I shift more, and Sir only uses more of his body weight to pin me into position. He leans into my body, immobilising me, and holding me tight against the tabletop, I feel the sharp sting of the large needle piercing my skin. It makes me cry out in an exaggerated whimper. There's a click and my buttock feels like it's on fire, then a cotton ball is held firmly against my skin where it has just been penetrated by the needle.

After a few minutes, Thomas discards the cotton and grabs his chip reader. He waves it over my buttock, and it dings, making everyone present aware that it has found a microchip. I am branded forever as someone else's pet. Someone else's dog, for as long as the chip remains in my buttock.

My head spins, full of thoughts of what has been said and the implications of what has been done. Thomas packs up his bag, and I'm brought back to reality.

"She needs to be trained daily, Owen. If she's going to accept what she is, it's vital."

Sir nods. "Thanks, Thomas. I appreciate it."

Thomas nods too. "When she's ready, let me know," he says cryptically. Sir lifts me down from the table and walks Thomas to the door.

"See you again soon," Thomas says, shaking Sir's hand.

"Thanks again, Thomas. I'll be in touch."

Thomas pats my head. "You be a good little bitch. I'll be back."

Sir waves Thomas off and then closes the door. He takes me over to the corner to a large doggie bed. He pushes me into the bed and unclips my leash.

"Stay," he warns before patting my head. "Good girl, Ginger." He smiles before walking off.

I curl up as best as I can with a painful buttock. Soon, I doze off and dream of chasing a tennis ball across a deserted beach.

Chapter Four

I'm sitting in the corner of Master O's living room, in my usual position. I'm naked, my wrists and ankles have leather restraints, my nipples have clamps with little bells on them, and there's a collar around my neck. I sit with my bottom resting on my feet, my legs parted, and my palms flat on my thighs. I don't look at him, my eyes cast firmly to the floor.

Sir is moving around, setting things up, and I try not to let my mind run away with me over what he has planned for me this evening. He finally gets his spanking bench in a position he wants it in, and he looks at me and grins, catching me looking in his direction. I quickly avert my eyes again, knowing it's too late and I've been busted.

"I saw you, girl. But with what I have in store for you this evening, I think I'll let you get away with it, just this once." He grins, and as he does, the doorbell rings. Sir goes to the door, and I listen carefully to what is happening. Before I realise what's going on, I hear Sir asking whomever it is to come in. Panic sets in. My heart starts to race, and I feel my cheeks flush with colour, a hue that then seeps down my body. He's about to bring someone else into the house while I'm sitting here naked and ready to be used.

It's something Master O and I had talked about; the inclusion of other dominants in our playtime, but it wasn't something I was aware of him organising. I know when it was discussed, it was mentioned that it would be something I, aside from the use of my safe word, would have no control over. Once again, it's proven how much Master O listens to what I say, and just how much he plans to take all my fantasies and make them a reality.

The living room door opens, and Sir walks in, followed by two of his friends. I close my eyes and take a deep breath to silence the pounding of my heart in my ears. "Adam, James. This is Emma. She's my submissive little slut, and she's here for us to use this evening in any way we see fit," Sir announces to them, pointing in my direction.

One of Sir's friends claps his hands together in delight. "So, this is the little one you've been telling us so much about."

Sir puts his hand on his friend's shoulder. "Adam," he says, warning him. "Don't leer. It's not polite." He laughs.

My cheeks burn more, and my pussy clenches at what might be in store for me. I'm wet and ready, and yet so incredibly nervous about what might happen next. Adam, James, and Sir settle themselves on the sofa and Sir looks at me. "Girl, go and get our guests some drinks," he commands, and I quickly stand and walk to the kitchen. I get Sir's favourite drink, scotch on the rocks, for him and his guests. I come back in and hand over each drink. When I go to return to my space in the corner, Sir stops me.

"Kneel," he commands, and I sink to the floor in front of the three men. "Hands on your head," he orders, and again, I do as I'm told. He uses his foot to push my legs further apart before rubbing the toe of his boot into my crotch, pushing it into my wet pussy, and rubbing it along my clit a few times before dropping his foot back to the floor.

"Look at the state of my boot, you dirty little whore. You've got it all slicked up. Get down there and clean that up," he growls at me. I drop my hands from my head and nervously lean forward on all fours, extending my tongue out to lick my juices from the leather.

As I clean Sir's boot, a firm hand strikes my backside. A hand I know is not Sir's strokes over my warmed skin before being removed, and another smack connects with my upturned ass. "She's got a very spankable arse," Adam purrs and runs his finger along my sex. I try to keep focused on Sir's boot as Adam's finger strays between my labia and is pushed into my pussy in one move.

Adam begins to fuck me with his fingers as I keep licking Sir's boot. Sir pulls on my collar to lift me from the floor. He unzips his jeans and pulls me over his crotch. His hard cock springs free and he pushes my face down onto it. I feel someone moving behind me, and another set of hands roam over my body as Sir begins to fuck my face, while Adam's fingers plunder my pussy. James's hands reach around me and grope my breasts, and all my senses are on overload as I come over Adam's hand.

"I think she likes your fingers, Adam," Sir breathes, clearly liking what I'm doing as much as I'm liking what Adam is doing. Adam adds an extra digit and keeps thrusting in and out of my soaked sex. I can feel Sir twitch in my mouth. I run my tongue along the underside of his thick cock and am rewarded with a hot mouthful as he explodes. I suckle gently, licking everything from him, feeling my own climax building again.

My hair is grabbed, I'm pulled from Sir's cock, and my

face is pushed down on another. James fists his hands in my hair and thrusts his cock into my throat. I gag, and my eyes start to water. I glance up, begging him with my eyes to ease off, even a little. Instead. he grins and pushes me further. James moves to the sofa, using my hair to keep me tightly over his dick. I glance at Sir and see the lust shining in his eyes. He's enjoying me being used by other men, and something within me makes me want to keep him pleased and lustful. I force myself to breathe through my nose and take James's cock as deeply as I can.

Adam's fingers continue to thrust into my pussy, and another orgasm threatens to engulf me again. My head starts to swim between climaxing and attempting to control myself over James's cock. I feel myself letting go of the last bit of nerves, letting the physical pleasure and emotional satisfaction in pleasing my Master take over.

James pushes deep, stopping at the back of my throat at the same time Adam cracks his hand down on my ass. I jolt, and James is allowed to breach the barrier into my throat. I gag, and James's hold on my hair tightens. I feel Sir's hands on my skin, rubbing my back, encouraging me without words. I know by how his fingertips cover my skin that he's proud of me, that he's turned on by me, that I'm in control and free to give my safe word if I need to. I can *feel* it in every movement of his fingers on my sizzling flesh.

Tears roll over my cheeks, and as Sir's fingers finally roam over my nipples, I explode over Adam's fingers one more time, and James rewards me with a choking flood of hot cum down the back of my throat. He pulls his semi-erect cock from my mouth with a pop, and Adam lets his hand fall from my pussy. I am allowed to sit back on my heels, my heart pounding, my sex soaked, and my breathing erratic. When I glance at Sir, the look in his eyes settles me and he grins. His hand rubs over my shoulder, and I breathe deeply. I can feel him regarding me closely. I know he's taking in everything, analysing me, making sure I'm still okay with the situation I've found myself in at his insistence.

Master O takes my hand and leads me over to the spanking bench.

"Do it," he whispers in my ear. I don't need any further instruction than that. I stand to position myself over the bench, careful to line myself up as Sir has trained me to.

Once I've lowered myself into position, Sir circles me, locking me into place with a restraint on each limb. My thighs are held apart, my ankles also, my pussy and ass exposed. My arms are bound at the wrists, my tits falling through a conveniently positioned hole in the bench, allowing them to be freely accessed at any time.

Master O takes a blindfold from a table nearby and covers my eyes, plunging me into darkness, unable to see who is touching me, not knowing whose cock is being forced into me.

I take a breath before hands are on my breasts, pulling on my clamps, the attached little bells jingling with the constant manipulation. As I moan in pleasure at the sensation, a cock is pushed against my lips. I open wider and allow it to penetrate my mouth completely. It pushes back against my throat, and I try to breathe through my nose and fight my gag reflex. Its owner pushes hard into my throat before pulling back and thrusting back in just as hard.

I jump when I feel a cock at the entrance to my soaked pussy. I groan loudly as the cock enters me with a slow and steady pace until I'm completely impaled. The hard cock pushing deep inside me pulses before pulling back and ramming deep inside me once more.

I moan as my body starts to tremble with the overload of sensation: my body, pussy, and mouth filled, hands on my breasts and nipples, on my hips, digging into my flesh, a hand in my hair controlling me. I am being thoroughly used, and I'm on the brink of coming apart for the most fantastic orgasm of my life.

My stomach tightens, my pussy starts to pulse, and a cataclysmic climax rips through me. I cry out as my mouth and throat are filled with cum and lick greedily as the cock is pulled from between my lips.

The cock in my pussy is pulled out, and I hiss at the sensation. I hear movement around me before my mouth is presented with another cock. From the taste of it, the one that was deep in my cunt moments before.

"You're doing great, little one," I hear Sir saying somewhere near my rear. "Keep control while I spank you! No biting!"

Just as the cock touches the back of my throat, a paddle connects with my backside. Being blindfolded adds just enough of the element of surprise that I lose the focus needed to breathe through my nose. I gag on the cock in my mouth and my teeth graze it as it pulls back.

There's a hiss and a throaty lust-filled voice, "Dammit, O. Your pet's teeth are sharp!"

I can hear Sir chuckle behind me. "Don't worry, Adam. She'll pay for it later!" The dick is pulled from my mouth at the time an extra hard crack from the paddle connects again with my buttocks. A fiery sting burns through my skin invoking a yelp, and as I cry out, the hard cock is again pushed deep into my mouth.

The pattern of paddle and deep throating continues

until I have lost all track of how many strikes my sensitive flesh has taken, and I'm left with only a deep sting in my ass with a burn that has spread to my pussy.

Sir's hand smooths over my ass cheeks, soothing me yet causing the skin to prickle with pain at the contact all the same. I feel the cool trickle over my ass as a digit spreads it over my tight asshole.

I groan as the digit presses into my ass, teasing me. The cock in my mouth pulses, and I hear Adam voice his appreciation. "Jesus, O. She liked that, and fuck, so did I!"

The digit is joined by another, and I moan around the cock again. It jumps in my mouth, and I know he's close. The fingers are slipped from my ass, and a cock is pushed against me in their place.

As the cock enters my ass, I buck against my restraints. I'm not in any pain, I'm on sensory overload. To Adam, with his cock in my mouth, it all proves too much, and I am rewarded with another mouthful of cum.

I swallow all I am given and lick the cock thoroughly before it slips from my mouth. I'm left with just the biting in my nipples from my clamps, my burning buttocks, and a filled and stretched asshole as Sir fucks me balls deep.

Another orgasm is quickly building within me. As I start to feel my ass twitching with an impending climax, hands grab my clamps and pull them from my nipples. There is a delicious burn of pain as the blood flows freely into them again. I scream out with abandon as my orgasm slams into me.

He holds my hips tightly and bucks his against me in a hard, unyielding pace. I'm not allowed to come down from my first orgasm this way as I'm caught by a second, and then a third in quick succession.

I'm vaguely aware of movement around me, but my

euphoria won't allow my brain to focus on anything. A final orgasm approaches, and Master O explodes within me, roaring as he does, barely audible over my own screams of pleasure.

Moments pass and I am aware of the sensation of my back being stroked as I start to come back down. Sir slides his spent cock from my ass, and he disappears from my backside, his hands moving from limb to limb, releasing me.

He helps me back off the spanking bench to rest on my heels. I feel the slickness everywhere between my legs, my jaw aches, and my body is weak. His lips connect with mine in a slow and tender kiss.

"I'm so proud of you." I can hear him smile and he removes the blindfold from my eyes.

We are alone again in his house. There is no sign of the friends who had been here moments before. He stands, scoops me into his arms, and takes me upstairs to the bathroom. I am bathed, caressed, and cared for before being carried to Sir's king-size bed, where I fall instantly into a sated sleep in Owen's arms.

Chapter Five

It's been about a month since Master O made me his bitch, quite literally. I have spent hours every day being his little pet, playing fetch, barking at the postman, trotting around after him on my leash. The more I do, the more and more I slip into that delicious headspace where everything else falls away, and all I am and want to be is Ginger. I have made sufficient progress that I no longer have to wear my hateful tongue gag. I know my place and what's expected of me.

I'm lying in my doggie bed, just lazing and thinking about the new toy Sir bought me, when there's a knock on the back door. I lift my head and sit up, ready to bark. The door knocks again, and I stand on all fours and start to growl.

"Ginger!" Master O scolds.

I stop and trot after him towards the door to see who is invading my territory. When Sir opens the door, I see the vet standing there. I glare at him, and he starts to laugh.

"I see you remember me, Ginger," he says and pats my head. I clench my ass and feel my tail start to wag. "You might like me this time. I've brought you something to play with," he tells me before pulling on the leash I didn't realise he had in his hand, and another dog appears. I creep forward a little, sniffing the air around the other dog. It moves towards me, and I bark.

"Ginger!" Sir scolds again. "Be nice!" He grabs my collar and pulls me back from the door, allowing the vet and the other dog the space to come into the kitchen. Once the back door is shut, the vet unclips the other dog's leash and allows him to come towards me. I can't help but growl at the stranger in my house. The other dog bows his head and barks at me, and suddenly I think they might be okay. I might be able to let them play fetch with me or just generally run around with them.

I creep forward and sniff at them again. Sir offers the vet a coffee, while they watch us get to know each other. The other dog rubs his nose against mine, smelling me before taking a smell of my skin the whole way down my side. I follow his actions and smell along his skin. The other dog smells good; there is a scent that makes my skin prickle, and somehow, my pussy moistens. When I reach the dog's hip, I can see he's a large male. His nose reaches my back end, and I feel him pressing it against my pussy and can feel his breath on my skin. I nudge his hip with my nose and watch his tail wag. I run my own nose across his backside. The same sweet scent tickles my nose. I think this is definitely a dog I can play with.

I turn to walk off into the living room, and the vet's dog trots along after me. "This should work out well," I hear the vet telling Sir.

Sir agrees. "They seem to naturally be getting on well anyway." He looks at me. "Do you like Duke, Ginger?" he asks me, and I wag my tail and bark to show my approval.

Sir smiles and pats my head and Duke's and lifts my favourite toy before walking back to the door. I trot along behind him with Duke following me. Sir throws my tennis ball outside and I rush out after it, hoping to get to it before Duke. Duke bounds out after me and gets there faster, lifting my ball in his mouth and rushing back to the back door.

It's not until I turn around that I notice Sir has closed the door and left us in the backyard together. Duke drops my toy at the back doorstep and trots back over to me. He nudges my cheek with his nose, and I bark at him, bouncing on my front paws, ready to play. His tail wags and he jumps at me, knocking me onto my side. I roll on my back and use my front paws to pat at his chest. His paws are at either side of my head, and he nudges at my exposed chest, his teeth finding my peaked nipples as he playfully nips at my skin. I yelp, roll back to my paws, and growl at him before I bounce at him with my front paws, and he barks back. I bounce again and Duke falls over. I waste no time in putting my mouth to his neck, nipping at his skin, letting him know who is alpha.

"GINGER!" Comes the scold from the back door. I look up to see the vet shouting at me. I release Duke and trot to the door, leaving him to get up and follow me. "Get in!" the vet scolds.

I trot into the house and Duke comes with me. Sir clips my leash back on my collar and pulls me into the living room behind him. He settles himself on the sofa and pulls on my leash before putting it under his foot, so I'm stuck and can't move.

The vet comes in after Sir and moves behind me. He has a little jar in his hand. He opens it before dipping a finger into it and then smearing it over my entrance. A heat starts to burn into me.

"Duke!" the vet calls, and his dog trots in on his command. Sir unclips my leash again, and I involuntarily wriggle at the feeling spreading through my sex.

Duke trots over behind me, and the vet nudges him in the direction of my backside. I feel Duke's nose at my ass, and his tongue licks a long, wet stroke over my sex. I yelp and turn away from him. When I do, I can see that whatever the vet put on me has Duke excited, his thick hard cock bobbing between his legs.

I'm startled by the sight and again move away from him, but Duke follows me, clearly attracted by whatever coats my backside. Again, his nose nudges against my ass, and his tongue takes another long lick of my sex. I'm soaked and inexplicably turned on, as though whatever balm has been applied is purely there to set my nerves on fire.

Duke takes delight in repeatedly rubbing his tongue in long strokes over my sex. I want to move, but the desire is taking over; I want more of his tongue instead. I stay still and let him work my soaked sex into more of a fury. I fidget and open my hind legs to allow Duke better access, and a whimper escapes from my mouth.

Before I know it, Duke's on my back, his cock bobbing against my pussy. I'm suddenly painfully aware of what's going on. I remember the vet's words on his first visit about me being a breeding bitch, and fear takes over. I move, causing Duke to stumble off my back. Everything in me wants to get up and move away from Duke on two legs. But I glance at Sir and see the look on his face and the bulge in his jeans; I know that this is what he wants, this is something that would please him.

Torn between what to do next—move away from Duke

or satisfy something Sir wants—I freeze. Duke takes that as his cue to mount me again. His skin is warm, and his chest covers my back. Again, his cock bobs at my entrance. He licks my shoulder and bites into my flesh as I flinch against him. My hind legs open a touch wider again, and he pushes his hips against me. The first time, his cock finds my pussy but slips past. The second time, however, Duke's cock sinks into my pussy, and he begins to buck against me, his dick thrusting back and forth into me. His hold on my shoulder causes a pain that seems to make my clit sizzle more. It's not long before I'm panting, on the edge of orgasm. Duke continues to pound into me, hard and frantic. I clench and pulse around him as my climax surges through me. Duke starts to growl, and his cock pulses and explodes inside me. The second he's done, Duke pulls out of me and lets his cock and cum slip from my slit. His nose returns to my pussy as he licks the length of me again, lapping at his own juices mixed with my own.

The vet and Duke stay at Sir's house the rest of the day. I lose count of the number of times Duke takes me. But by the end of the day, I'm actively encouraging him, nudging his ass with my nose before running my tongue over his balls, seeking him out to mount me and fuck me.

As they leave, Sir pats my head. "You did well today, Ginger," he praises. "It looks like you're not just my bitch anymore, though. Looks like you're Duke's bitch too." He grins at me. Knowing this pleases him pleases me. I walk tenderly back over to my bed in the dining room, settling down, my pussy still filled with Duke and very sensitive from the bout of rutting that was done to me. Again, I doze off, this time dreaming of the next time I might be able to see Duke.

Chapter Six

It's been about eight months since I started playing with Owen and experimenting in the BDSM lifestyle. We have played a lot, and our relationship both as Dominant and submissive has changed, as has our friendship. He told me he felt that he wants to test me. Apparently, he thinks it's something I'm ready for. It thrills me and makes me nervous all at the same time. I want so much to please him, but at the same time, I worry he's picking something that's going to push me too far.

I take a deep breath and knock on Owen's door. He smiles sweetly when he sees me.

"Come in, little one." He grins and kisses me softly. 'Don't worry, I have faith in you," he tells me, reading me perfectly without me having to say a single word to him. That element of our relationship is new to me, to have someone capable of understanding me so completely, to read me, to be inside my head and see my thoughts and fears so clearly. It's a strangely comforting experience now that I'm over the initial unnerving feeling it gave me.

Master O ushers me into his living room, where he has

the spanking bench set up and ready for me. He smiles at me and rubs his fingers along my arms.

"Strip," he commands and places a kiss on my neck.

I follow his command without hesitation and stand with my hands by my sides. His hands roam over my skin.

"You know I want to test you, don't you, little one?" he asks.

"Yes, Sir," I reply softly.

"You know that all you have to do is say your safe word, don't you, pet?"

I nod. "Yes, Sir."

He smiles and puts a finger under my chin to tilt my head towards him. "Good," he whispers against my lips before kissing me tenderly.

He takes my hand and leads me to the spanking bench. I drape myself over it as I have done countless times before, and Sir circles me, securing me tightly to the bench. He strokes his hand down my back before spanking my ass hard. I flinch with a groan at the contact. Sir comes back round towards my head and gathers my hair in his hand, pulling my head up. With his free hand, he unbuttons and unzips his jeans and frees his stiffening cock, pressing it at my lips.

I open my mouth and allow him to slide his cock across my tongue, and I close my lips around him and suck. Sir grows harder in my mouth and starts to thrust into my throat. His firm hand in my hair and his forcefulness in taking my mouth make me wet, and I show him with the enthusiasm with which I flick my tongue over his shaft. Sir uses my mouth as he needs to, moaning as his cock starts to pulse in my mouth, and his hips buck against my face with a little less control. My eagerness is rewarded when Master O explodes down my throat with a loud groan.

Sir stoops to lick the taste of himself from my lips with a kiss. I moan against his mouth, turned on by his demands of me this far. He moves to my rear, and I am quickly rewarded with his tongue lapping at my wet labia. He nuzzles his face against me before his tongue swirls over my clit. The situation has me so primed; it isn't long before that delicious feeling starts to brew low in my belly. When Sir's tongue swirls around my asshole, I cry out as a climax hits me. His finger continues to work my clit as his tongue sweeps over my ass, and his teeth suddenly sink into my buttock as he bites me hard.

A second orgasm takes over me as Sir plunges two of his long fingers into my soaked pussy, his thumb still circling my clit.

"I love how wet you get for me, my little slut," he teases against my buttocks as he curls his fingers inside me. He's been slipping more and more verbal humiliation into our play, and I have to admit it's been more of a turn-on than I ever thought possible. I love hearing him call me names. I moan as he rubs over my G-spot and continues to taunt me. His free hand strokes over my back and reaches for my nipples and breasts through the gap in the spanking bench, and again, I climax over his hand.

I'm aware of how he's working me a lot, and it makes me a little apprehensive about what he has coming. That nervousness mixed with his actions makes me wetter, my head spinning with possibilities. He brings me out of my thoughts with a firm twist of my nipple.

"You're ready for it, aren't you, my little slut?" he asks.

I have no idea what he's asking me if I'm ready for, but I know whatever it is, I want it, and I want it now. He pulls his hand from my pussy, and I groan out in frustration.

"I'm going to push you, my little pet. I'm going to test

you, and if you pass, then I might just have a reward for you," he tells me. I look up at him and want nothing more than to prove to him that I am ready for whatever test he has. Whatever he wants to push me with, I will accept his challenge.

"Please, Sir," I say, and I can see from his grin that he is happy with my reaction. He pulls a blindfold from his pocket and places it over my eyes, kissing my cheek as he does.

"Good girl," he whispers against my ear, and I shiver at the sensation it raises in me. His hands are again on my breasts, groping them roughly and pulling on my nipples. Suddenly, I feel the nip of nipple clamps, but ones I have only had a few times. These have teeth; mean little crocodile clips that bite into my tender flesh. I wriggle against my restraints, every inch of my body suddenly super sensitive to any stimuli. I feel Sir at my ass and wonder what is coming next.

"You're not gagged. If you need to use your word, do so," he reminds me before landing a paddle against my ass. I jump at the unexpected jolt, and my pussy clenches at the thought of him paddling me repeatedly, more than he ever has before, wondering if that is to be my test. He continues to strike my ass, over and over, at least ten times before stopping. A vibrator is placed against my clit, and I am teased. My body responds to his attention on my clit, and I start to shiver with another impending orgasm. As I approach that point, the vibrator disappears, and the paddle returns to connect with my buttocks.

Master O repeats this pattern over and over. Pushing me to the brink of orgasm, only to force me back down with the paddling of my ass. I have no idea how long he has been doing this because my frustration has taken over, and I just want to come. He paddles me again and tears start to fall from my eyes. I'm so desperate for release that I can't take it anymore.

Sir stops paddling my backside and strokes over my enflamed skin. My ass is burning, and so are my pussy and clit. Needy, wanton, and every single touch from him just makes me worse. He pushes something cold and wet against my asshole, and I assume it's a plug coming. Sir slowly pushes the plug into my backside, and I groan, needing more. My ass is smacked again, and I clench around the new plug. Suddenly I'm aware of a new sensation. My asshole is starting to tingle and burn.

"Can you feel that?" Sir asks, and I can hear his smile.

"Yes, Sir!" I reply breathlessly.

"That's a finger of ginger, my dirty little girl. It's going to burn for about twenty minutes or so, and I'm going to enjoy torturing you even more while it's there. If you clench, you'll make it worse on yourself. Understand?" he asks.

I nod. "Yes, Sir." I try not to clench the ginger root finger that's buried in my ass; every time I do, I feel the extra burn. Sir's fingers are in my wet slit, and he pushes something against my clit.

"That's ginger too, slut. You're going to like how it makes you feel," he tells me, and with that, his contact with me disappears.

The constant tingle in my ass grows into a burn. My clit is tingling, and I can't help but want to wriggle, needing more. I clench in need and the burn intensifies instantly. I cry out with a groan, and I hear a chuckle nearby. A second later there is a pull on my nipples. I'm vaguely aware of what he's done, he's clipped weights on the clamps on my tits. I groan more. I need to come; my frustrations are at a fever pitch. I feel desperate like never before for an orgasm, to be fucked, to climax. I am beyond needy.

I hear another chuckle and feel Sir whisper near my ear, "That's the ginger, little slut. It makes you a wanton little whore. You'll be begging me to fuck you by the time I'm done with you."

Another slow, agonised groan escapes from me, and I'm compensated with a spank on the backside. Again, I clench my ass involuntarily at the contact, which elicits an intense burn that borders on painful for my actions. The feelings are intense. It's overwhelming and overpowering, and I almost want to scream out and beg for him to free me and fuck me every way he can, but I don't want to give in. I don't want to let myself down, never mind Master O.

I have no idea how much time passes, but Sir mixes the stimulation between the paddling of my backside, the pulling on my nipples, and the constant presence of the ginger in my ass and on my clit. My mind is spinning; I can't focus on a single thought. I've regressed to a moaning little whore with only one blinding need; to be fucked hard and to come. It's a need so great that it's practically painful. The burning in my backside is subsiding, and I don't know if it's because it's naturally wearing off or because everything else is so overriding it pales in comparison.

Sir fists my hair in his hand, and his cock is pressed against my lips. He pushes it hard, forcing it back towards my throat. "Is this what you want?" he gloats over me before fucking my face hard for several minutes.

I choke and nod as he pulls out of my mouth. "Yes, Sir!" I gasp, and my mouth is filled with his dick once again.

"Beg for it," he commands me this time as he pulls it from my face again.

"Please, Sir. *Please!* I *need* to come. I want your cock," I whine, my mouth filled with cock again the second I pause. He thrusts between my lips, hitting the back of my throat each time. He's teasing me more. It's what I want, but it's not where I need it the most. I moan over his length and wriggle in my restraints. The movement sets the weights swaying on my nipples, stimulating me further. He yanks himself from my mouth with a pop, tugging hard on my hair.

"Stay still!" he warns.

"*Please*, Sir," I beg. I don't care anymore; I need it. I need to feel him deep in my pussy.

Master O moves away from me, releasing my hair. He unclips the weights on my nipples, leaving them still clamped. He moves behind me, flicks the ginger from my clit, and then slowly pulls the ginger plug from my ass. I groan. As much as it caused an unpleasant sensation, the removal of the only thing that was filling me leaves me feeling bereft. His hands land on my backside, and his thumbs pull my labia apart, exposing me further. Seconds later, his cock is thrusting deep inside me in one single stroke.

I cry out as Sir sets a punishing pace, fucking me hard, his fingers digging into my hips as he drives into me over and over, racing me to the edge of a cliff, ready to jump off into a tidal wave of orgasmic bliss. I feel it starting; the pull in my lower stomach, the tingling in my clit, and just as I think I'm about to shatter into a million pieces, Sir withdraws from my body and smacks my arse hard.

I whimper, and tears fall from my cheeks. I can't take it anymore. I want to come; I need to more than I need to even breathe at this very moment. Sir moves in front of me and pulls my blindfold off. I look up at him and I'm overwhelmed by the look on his face. His eyes are swimming with lust, but he looks genuinely tender and caring; pride and love shine from his face as he looks at me and his hand goes into his pocket.

"I want to do something else. Do you trust me?" he asks.

I answer without a second of hesitation, "Yes, I trust you, Sir." He smiles and removes his hand from his pocket. He shows me what he has. It's a collar with a little metal plate riveted on it. 'Property of Master O' is engraved on the plate. A small padlock goes with it. I smile up at him and nod. He slips the collar around my neck and locks the padlock. He pulls a small dog tag-style necklace from the collar of his t-shirt and shows me the key for the padlock.

"We can sort a less obvious one for when we're not in scene. But I want you, little one. I want to keep you as mine, look after you, challenge you. To watch you grow in your submission," he explains.

I smile broadly up at him. We had talked about the concept, but never in terms of it happening between us. Who would have known you could want something so much, despite having given it no thought before?

"Now you can have what you want." He grins, moving behind me again and thrusting back into my pussy in one movement.

I groan. Warmth floods me, not only from the orgasm that's quickly building within me again, but because Owen, the man and the master, wants me around, to care for me, to nurture my submission, to do what he is doing right now, driving me to an earth-shattering orgasm. The world around me disappears as my climax crashes into me, made even more intense by the knowledge that I am his... I am owned.

THE END

Seduced

'To torture a man you have to know his pleasures.'

Chapter One

It doesn't normally happen this way, but when I see him, the attraction is something I just can't ignore. There is just something about him that lures me to him when I see him across the hotel bar. It doesn't take long before we're in the lift, heading for his room. The temptation is too much, and as soon as the lift doors close, I pounce, forcing him up against the wall of the elevator car, pushing his hands above his head and crushing my lips to his. His fingers link with mine as I hold his hands above his head, grinding my body against his as my tongue hungrily fucks his mouth. He growls deep in his chest and pushes back against me, forming his body to mine, letting me feel his length against my stomach, inviting me for more.

When the lift dings, announcing we have arrived at his floor, I push myself off him, keeping one hand locked with his, and pull him behind me. "Room number?" I demand seductively.

"Three-oh-nine," he replies, and I pull him in the direction of his room.

Once at the door, I tuck myself in behind him, slipping

my hand into his pocket and getting his key. I let my hand rummage into his pocket deeply, stroking along his length and fondling his balls. He sighs and lifts his arms, leaning in against the door, supporting himself as I play with him through his pocket. He bites his bottom lip to stifle a moan, and I pull my hand from his trousers and wave the key at him, putting it in the lock and opening the door.

Secure on the other side, I again launch myself against him, pushing him against the wall, his hands back over his head, and my lips back on his. I push my feet between his and manoeuvre his legs apart. I take the tie around his neck in my hand and tug on it; it loosens in my grasp. I break the kiss to look at the knot on the tie as I untie it, tugging it from around his neck. He looks at me through eyes hooded with desire and holds his hands out in front of him. I slip the tie around his outstretched wrists and bind them together tightly. He puts them back above his head and leans in for another kiss.

I respond to him greedily, my lips crushing against his, my tongue lapping over his as they dance together in our mouths. I want this man, and what's more, I want him naked. Hell, I want us both naked, the temptation to have my bare nipples pressed against his broad chest is just too much to resist. I pull his shirt free from his pants and start to undo the buttons. I move my lips from his, nibbling along his jaw until I reach his neck. A moan slips from his lips as my mouth makes contact with the tender skin just below his ear. I stop, lifting my head to look at him. I stare at him, keeping direct eye contact while I undo the rest of his buttons and flick the sides of his shirt apart, exposing his chest roughly. I run my hand across his jaw, over his lips, and down his masculine chest with a smattering of dark, dirty fair hair, right down to the little happy trail that leads into the front of his pants with the promise of something enticing. He sucks in a breath and holds it as my fingers go lower.

We both look down as I skim my palm over his swollen crotch, his held breath coming out in a throaty moan. I crush my lips against his again. My hands reach for his bound wrists, still above his head as I press my still-covered breasts against him, the friction of contact and fabric making my nipples stiffen to hard little pebbles. My hands move to his bare sides, grabbing at his skin, needing him closer as his own hands drop. He loops his restrained arms around my back, pulling me tighter against him.

Encased in his bound arms and flat against his chest, I can't resist when he nibbles my bottom lip and then nuzzles against the skin on my neck. I groan at the sensations washing over me, wanting more of him. I need to take back control and I break contact from him, dipping and ducking out from underneath his looped arms.

"Ah, ah, ah!" I scold, reaching for the hem of my top. "Do you want to see more?" I ask him, pausing with my top gathered, ready to pull off.

"You know I do," he replies huskily.

"Arms!" I warn, and he leans back against the wall and puts his arms back over his head, waiting. I lick my lips and slowly pull the top off over my head, dropping it to the floor. His inky black eyes sparkle with lust, and I reach behind me to unhook my bra. When I let it slip from my shoulders and down my arms, he hums in appreciation at seeing my ample breasts spill free. His breathing speeds up, and I slowly move in, brushing against him again, my nipples gently tickled by his chest hair. I skim myself against him, bare chest to bare breasts, and my lips lock with his once more, my hands again at his sides, pulling him towards me. I need to feel him closer.

As his tongue tangles with mine, again, his arms come down around me, and he pulls me tight against him. His lips trace across mine and to my neck and bare shoulder. He nibbles my skin, sucking it harshly into his mouth. He's marking me. I dig my nails into his back, and he bites down harder with a low moan, keeping me pressed against him.

"Mmmm... That's not how this is meant to work!" I warn him on an aroused sigh.

He lifts his head and looks at me with a smirk. "You can punish me for it later!"

I reach up for his head and grab a fistful of hair. "Oh, I will. You can bet on it!"

"I'm counting on it!"

I pull his head back, tuck my hands under his arms, and shove them back over his head away from me. I take a step back, letting my eyes roam over him. He shoots me a predatory look and lets his eyes feast on me in return.

I grin and walk away from him towards the bed. He looks at me when I pause and turn back to him.

"Crawl," I command.

He holds out his bound wrists as though they explain everything. I shrug and look at him again. "Crawl."

He keeps his back against the wall, kicks off his shoes, and sinks to his knees. His eyes never leave mine as he does. He finally comes to rest at my feet and again holds his hands out to me expectantly.

I take a step back from him and look at him intently. "I'm not sure you can be trusted to behave without your hands bound!"

He raises his eyebrows suggestively, and my pussy clenches. Shit, this guy is trouble: submissive with a hot streak of defiant alpha. A positively explosive combination. I hold his look before stepping toward him and reaching for his bound wrists. I untie him, slipping the tie around the back of my neck, keeping it to hand, just in case.

"Shirt off," I instruct, and his shirt slips off his body, gracing me with an unobstructed view. He is glorious. A broad chest and shoulders, toned without being obviously muscular, and a dappling of body hair a fraction darker than that on his head. He rubs a hand across his chest absently and looks up at me through thick lashes. The intensity of his gaze takes my breath away, and for a split second; I forget just how much I want control.

"And the rest," I tell him.

He grins. "And you," he insists.

"Together," I state in compromise and reach for the waist of my skirt, unzipping it. He reaches for his fly. Undoing the buttons on his jeans, he pulls them down his hips, over his legs to the floor before kicking them to the side. I let my skirt drop and pool at my feet.

We both stand there in our underwear, him in his tented cotton boxers and me in my lacy thong and stockings. He licks his lips as his eyes roam over my lower half before he takes a step towards me. He pauses before me, silently waiting for permission to do what he wants to. I gaze up at him and close the last of the space between us. I crush my lips against his. His hands find my ass and pull me tight against him, his hard cock pressing against my stomach.

As his tongue duels with mine, I wrap my arms around his neck. His hands grip my ass firmly and I'm hoisted up. Instinctively, my legs go around his hips as I cling on. His cock is now pressed hard against my throbbing pussy.

"This isn't how it's meant to go!" I breathe against his lips.

"So, stop me," he challenges and presses his lips to mine again. A fight begins inside me. The lust and the need I have for him versus the need to dominate and control. I'm really not sure which one I want to win more. I pull myself tighter against him and lose myself in the feeling of his lips on mine, his length against my sex, and how delicious this is.

His hands slide from my ass and up my back as he keeps a firm hold on me. With his arms encircling me, he backs up to the bed and collapses backwards, taking us both to the mattress. I pry myself off his chest and sit up on his hips, his cock still resting firmly against my wet sex.

"Do you trust me?" I grin at him.

His hands run over my stocking-covered thighs and come to rest on my hips, grabbing me as he grinds up against me. "Maybe." He smirks, quirking an eyebrow at me.

I slip the tie from around my neck again. "Wrists," I say as I hold the tie out in front of me, expecting him to put his arms out to me. He does. He smiles, and I wrap the tie around them, tying it tightly. I place them back on his stomach and lean over him, trapping them between us.

I kiss him hard and hungrily, letting him know exactly how I'm feeling. The lust I have bubbling over makes me feverish. I kiss across his jaw and down his neck. I nibble on his earlobe and delight in the growl that rumbles through him. It spurs me on, and I can't help but dig my teeth into his shoulder. He groans. "It's a good job you bound my hands, or I wouldn't be able to control myself right now," he warns. His appreciation of my actions only makes me bolder; I suck and nip at his flesh, marking him, claiming him as mine. He bites his lip and moans.

I release my mouth's hold on his shoulder and push myself up on his chest, grabbing his wrists before leaning back over him as I push them back over his head.

"You'd better behave," I warn him as I start to kiss my way down the side of his abdomen. He squirms beneath me. "Stay still!" I shoot him a glare.

He grins back at me. "It tickles!" He smiles and grinds his hips against me. I sink my teeth into his side, and a hiss erupts from him. I gaze in his direction and watch him watching me intently. I lift my head and warn again, "I told you to stay still."

"You're making it hard," he replies.

I grind against his hips, pressing myself tightly against his throbbing cock. "I know." I grin back at him and return to my kisses and nibbles along his side before moving to his mouth. I start with a lick across his lips, kissing down over his chin and neck, and then start to nip and suck across his chest muscles. Finally, my mouth reaches his right nipple, and I surround it, sucking it into my mouth. A rumbling growl resonates from him. He arches his back and meets my glance as I look up at him, his gaze heady with lust and full of desire. Warmth pools between my legs, and my lacy underwear is soaked. His stare is amplified, and I know he can feel the reaction he's creating in me too. "Don't you dare," I warn.

"You're testing my limits!"

"That's the idea." I smirk at him and move to his left nipple. He groans, and his hands move so his arms cover his face as he attempts to keep control of himself. I want to push him. I want him to make a move. I want to know just how much it will take. I want him to challenge me. I graze his nipple with my teeth, and I know what's coming a fraction of a second before it happens.

He lifts himself off the bed to sit up, taking me with him. His bound hands do nothing to stop him circling his arms around me. His mouth possesses me, and he pulls me tight against him. I melt in against him, my body naturally responding to his whether I want it to or not. Not that there's any doubt that I want it to. He grinds himself against me, and soon, my senses are swimming. Everything is lost other than my need for him.

"Untie me," he pants against my lips when he breaks our kiss. He unhooks his arms from around me and puts his hands in front of me expectantly. Normally, I would hesitate, but there is just something about him that prevents me from doing so. My fingers fumble against the knots in the tie as I try to get it off hastily. The instant his wrists are unbound, he runs his fingers through my long loose curls and pulls my face back to his as his lips possess mine once more.

I circle my arms around his waist, my nails digging into the skin on his lower back. His lips move across my face to my jaw before dipping to my neck. He instinctively finds that sweet spot below my ear, and my head falls back as I let out a moan. One hand runs down my back and sweeps around my waist before finding its home on my left breast.

His lips reach my shoulder, his hand kneading my breast. When he catches my nipple with his finger and thumb, his mouth's force on my shoulder increases. He's marking me like I marked him. Part of me wants to stop him, but the other part wants to surrender to the sensations he can generate in me, new and unbridled. I dig my nails hard into his flesh, not realising just how deeply until a hiss sounds from him, and his mouth releases my shoulder. "You're determined to leave marks, aren't you, kitten?" His nickname rings in my ears, and I lift my head to stare at him. "What's wrong?" he asks.

"Nothing, it's... silly."

He lifts his hand to my chin and kisses the tip of my nose. "It's not silly. Tell me."

I find his gaze comforting, and I want to explain. "You called me kitten, and my name is Kat. I'm Katriona," I tell him.

"You're such a little sex kitten. I just knew it would fit you." He smiles. "And for the record, I'm Mike. I'd like to hear my name on your lips when I make you come, my little Kat," he whispers before owning my mouth with his once more.

Suddenly, the space between us is too great. Our only barrier is our underwear, but it's too much and I can't take it. I push him back. I need to feel his skin against mine completely. I need to feel him—on me, in me. Placing a trail of kisses along his abdomen, I slowly make my way downward, tracing the line of hair from his belly button that disappears below the waistband of his underwear. I gaze up at him and pause, my fingers lightly resting at his hips, waiting for him to stop me.

"Do it," he replies to my unspoken question. I don't falter in pulling his boxers down over his hips and thighs; he lifts his ass from the bed to help me. He raises his feet and kicks them to the side. My eyes roam over the sight of him lying naked on the bed in front of me. His cock bobs against his stomach, as though he can feel my gaze like a soft caress. I'm hypnotised by it, unable to resist it. I have to taste him and dip my head towards him and run my tongue along his length. His warm, soft skin is a delight on my tongue, and I long to savour more of him. I lift him in my hand and cover the head of his cock with my mouth, sucking him between my lips and relishing in his aroused sighs. I bathe his dick in licks, exploring all over his head, lapping the pre-cum leaking from the tip.

I bob my head up and down in a slow, sensual, teasing pace, each time allowing a little more of him to push into my throat.

"Oh, Jesus, Kat!" he exclaims, grabbing my shoulders roughly. I gaze up at him, and his cock slides from my wet mouth.

Suddenly, I'm pinned to the bed on my back and my lacy knickers are gone, torn from my body in one swift move. He leans over me, pushing his knee between my legs. I stare into his eyes as my legs naturally part for him. He presses himself against me, resting on his elbows so we have skin-to-skin contact from our chest to our pelvis, to our tangle of legs.

"You're going to scream for me, little Kat," he says, brushing my hair from my face and nuzzling against my neck. "And when you do, you're going to scream my name," he breathes against my ear.

A shiver travels up and down my spine, and the tip of Mike's cock nudges between my slick folds. With a small move of his hips, he finds my entrance and slowly slides himself home.

I can't help myself. I wrap myself around him. I hook my legs around the back of his thighs, and my hands stroke up his sides and hold on to his broad shoulders and back. He rocks his pelvis against mine. I feel every last inch of him buried inside me, moving deeper, filling me until I'm sure I'm about to burst with ecstasy.

He bruises my lips with his own and captures my moans as if he needs them to breathe, kissing each one from me. He's slowly increasing his pace, the extra movement causing a tickle between my nipples and his chest hair. He's managing to rub across my clit with every stroke, and I find a furious storm brewing between my legs. His breathing is picking up. He's right there with me, feeling that need, that lust, chasing that finishing line.

Like a rising crescendo in a symphony, his hips thrust into me more and more. Finally, I just can't contain it any longer. Stars start at the edges of my vision until I'm swallowed by a blinding light as wave after wave of orgasm crashes over me.

"Fuck, Mike!" I scream out as he thrusts hard into me. I want to come down from the experience, but he doesn't stop.

"That's it, Kat," he pants against my lips. "One more," he encourages, and the split second I'm coming down is replaced by another cataclysmic climax.

I pull him tight against me as he stiffens. A roar erupts from him as he is captured by his own orgasm. He leans back against me and kisses me tenderly as we both lie there, basking in the afterglow of what happened. My hands caress his back, and he strokes the side of my face.

\-

After that night, I gave Mike my number. I always played safe men who were submissive, so the control was mine, but Mike is different. He's challenging, a little bit alpha male. As it turns out, he lives not far from me. We've seen each other a few times now. Who knows where things might lead?

Chapter Two

It's been a long time since I've had a man in my own home. I go to theirs, we have fun in hotels, but I've always tried to keep my sex life away from my personal space. So, having Mike here is a completely new experience for me. It's not the first time he's been in my house, but this is the first time he's been coming here exclusively for me to dominate him. There's something suddenly more intimate about the whole experience.

There's a knock at the door, and when I open it, he's standing there with a familiar cheeky grin on his face.

"Come in," I demand with a smirk, standing aside to let him in.

"Good evening, Mistress." He beams at me and plants a kiss on my cheek. I try not to smirk in the face of his impish charm. I know what he's doing, and I can't help but adore him for it. He's trying to lighten the mood and do as much as he can to make the experience easier on me.

"Strip," I command. He looks at me, and I know what he's thinking. "Yes, right here in the hallway."

Slowly, taking pleasure in teasing and flashing every last

inch of his skin, Mike starts to remove all of his clothing, just as he was told to, standing right there in my hall. When all of his glorious form is naked, he smiles and stands with his hands by his sides, daring me to look at all of him. I allow myself the indulgence, my eyes roaming over all of his form until my gaze finally reaches his impressive hard cock.

"On your knees," I demand.

He complies, never breaking his gaze from mine. He sinks down, his buttocks resting on his heels, looking up at me. I push my bare foot forward to him. "Kiss it," I tell him. He leans forwards and places his lips gently against the top of my foot. I glance down at him, and he catches the meaning in my raised eyebrow. He returns his attention to my foot and kisses it more tenderly, his tongue running along the side of my foot, and his lips nipping at my toes. I bite my bottom lip, enjoying the sensation already, desire moving from his lips on my feet directly to my pussy.

I pull that foot back and extend the other one for the same treatment. Mike wraps his lips around my toes and licks along my foot, and again, I feel every movement right through to my pussy. This man is already becoming my undoing. He's more than I had ever considered taking on previously. Both in the fact that he's not a typical submissive, and that I'm now out of my comfort zone having a man back in my house, getting under my skin, the same submissive to play with every time. The look he gives me as he rises on his knees and runs his hand up my inner leg and under my dress wipes away every hesitation. I grab his wrist and look at him with a hard stare.

"Excuse me? Were you invited to do anything other than kiss my feet?" I ask him.

He smirks at me, his eyes already full of lust. "No... *Miss*," he says, purposely pausing as if he had forgotten his place and needed to tack the last word on once he remembered.

"Is calling me your mistress causing you issues, little one?" I smile at him.

"It's not what I'd like to call you, Kitty Kat," he says defiantly. Something about how he rolls his tongue around my name makes me willing to forgive him and allow him this one concession.

"Fine," I concede. "As long as you show me respect as your dominant, I don't care what term you use to address me. But let's not overuse the 'Kitty Kat,' please."

He nods and sinks back until his butt rests on his heels again. "What would you like to do with me?" He smiles, holding his arms out to show himself off, his confidence coming off him in waves.

"Get upstairs." He goes to rise from his knees. "Ah! Ah! I didn't say you could get up now, did I?" The *are you kidding me* look he gives me is more reward than I had hoped for. He turns around on his hands and knees and crawls up the stairs as I commanded, with me following. I drink in the sight of his arse waving before me, and I know I'm going to enjoy making it a delicious shade of red.

He creeps up the stairs, and without asking, heads straight for my bedroom, with me admiring the view as he does. When he reaches beside the bed, he rests back on his heels and waits for me to say something more. I move to the large chest of drawers in the room, pull open the bottom drawer, and lift out my leather wrist and ankle restraints.

"On the bed. Face down," I instruct.

He rises, his hard cock standing proud in front of him, and he places himself onto the bed, face down, his head supported with his hand, his arm up on his elbow. He watches me as I move towards him with the restraints. I take the time to rub my fingers over his skin and place a chaste kiss against his inner wrists and ankles, buckling the cuffs tight.

He looks at me over his shoulder, silently asking what I'm going to do next. I move to the bottom of the bed and reach under the mattress, pulling out a sneaky little under-bed restraint system I have. I open the clip on his ankle cuff, connect it to the ring, and pull the strap tight, pulling Mike's ankle almost to the corner of the bed. I repeat the process on his other ankle, and then his two wrists. By the time I'm finished, he's a starfish, restrained tightly to the bed, face down. I stand beside him and let him watch as I strip out of my dress, bra, and knickers, letting them all fall to the floor as I delight in his lustful gaze.

"See anything you like?" I tease him.

"You know I do, kitten," he says on a sigh.

I grin at his admission of desire and walk towards the bed, climbing onto it, straddling him, and putting my backside down on top of his, my pussy perfectly in line with the crack of his arse. I grind myself against him, letting him feel that I'm already wet at the thought of having him here on my bed, naked. He groans when he feels my slickness against him. I lean over to him, my mouth by his ear, my breasts and stiff nipples pressed against his back. "Do you like that feeling?" I ask.

He moans. "Fucking right I do."

Now I begin the big tease.

I move against his back, making sure to trail the tips of my nipples against him. I start at his neck and plant a trail of soft kisses down under his ear, over his shoulder, and down his back. I kiss down along his side, knowing he's ticklish there, letting the heat of my breath blow across his skin. His ass muscles tighten, and he flexes against the bed. I lift my hand and give him a hard strike against his buttocks.

"Don't you dare dry hump my sheets, slut," I warn.

A soft growl ripples through Mike and causes goosebumps to rise on my skin. I have a need to find out just how much of a red arse he can handle now I see his reaction to my hand with a little name-calling. I move against him, changing my position, slipping down his back and coming to rest between his outspread legs. I can't resist giving his backside an extra slap as I do.

I lean forward, and I sink my teeth into his right buttock. I want to mark him, to brand him. I want to push him and see what he can take. I apply a gentle sucking pressure along with my teeth, knowing that a reddish-purple mark will rise on his skin. He moans, and again, his ass muscles tighten. I smack his left buttock.

I need to tease him, to tempt him, to prove submission is just what he needs. I run my hands along his inner thighs and crack them down hard on his ass cheeks. I repeat the action several times, caressing his thighs, soothing his skin, and increasing his need, fuelling my desires just as much as his.

After a few cycles of the tease, followed by the slaps, his ass is turning a nice shade of pink and starting to feel warm to the touch, but I know I can do better. I run my hands up his thighs again, and this time, instead of slapping his buttocks, I grab them firmly and spread them. His arsehole is exposed to me, and I lean forward and circle it with the tip of my tongue. Mike's initial jolt at the sensation quickly subsides to a low moan. His hips lift, and I feel him trying to move against my mouth.

I bury my face between his buttocks and lavish his arse with attention from my tongue. I can feel him moving against the bed. I know he's attempting to get the right kind of friction he needs to be able to jack himself off with my tongue fucking his arsehole, and it's the best reaction I could have hoped for. I stop and get off the bed. Mike groans and lifts his head to see what's going on.

"Kat?" he questions.

I grin. "Don't worry, I'm not done with you yet." I open a drawer and lift out three items: a butt plug, some lube, and a paddle. I move back to the bed, and I return to my position between Mike's legs.

"If you need me to stop, I will, okay?" I remind him.

"Do it, Kat!" he growls, lust filling his voice.

I rub my hand over his pink buttocks, open the lid on the lube, and dribble it between his ass cheeks. I rub my fingers down to his arsehole, pushing the lube against him, coating him.

I start to tease him, my lubed finger pushing into him, demanding entrance. The sound Mike makes when my index finger breaches that ring of muscle is beyond divine. It's a low, almost primal groan that makes my clit throb.

I spend a few moments fucking him with my finger, watching it with fascination as it disappears into him. After his hips attempt to fall into a rhythm with my finger, I smack him hard on the ass with my other hand.

"Stay still," I warn.

I rub the butt plug with some lube, with my spanking hand, and slip my finger from Mike's arse before replacing it with the butt plug. I'm done teasing, and I push it into his ass in one slow, firm movement. His previous guttural groan returns with new intensity, and the wetness of my pussy makes my thighs slick.

With the plug securely in place, I straddle Mike's restrained right leg and make sure he is very much aware of just how wet I am by rubbing my cunt on his leg, grinding it against him.

"Jesus, Kat..." he begins, but I don't let him finish the thought before I crack the paddle down hard on both buttocks. Mike hisses in pain, yet the flex of his hips afterwards suggests he's more turned on than I had hoped.

"You're a dirty little slut, aren't you?" I ask rhetorically. "I know how hard you are from having your ass filled, and now I'm going to punish you for it!" I inform him, shifting on his leg, reminding him of my wet pussy.

I begin paddling his ass further with earnest. I count each strike out loud, making sure almost every last one connects with the base of the butt plug, increasing the mixture of sensations Mike is experiencing.

By the time I've finished with the thirty lashes of the paddle, his arse looks like it's on fire it's so red, and Mike is writhing about on the bed seeking some kind of release. I move off the bed, putting the paddle away. I return to Mike's ankles and unclip them from the straps. I then do the same to his wrist cuffs. When I go to step back from the bed, Mike lunges, grabbing me and pulling me down on the bed beside him.

He puts me on my back and moves between my legs, using his body to cover mine, sinking his rock-hard dick into my cunt and his lips over mine to capture my groans of pleasure.

I fall asleep that night thoroughly sated, having been taken to the dizzying heights of orgasmic bliss several times by a hot alpha yet submissive male with a plugged arse.

Suddenly, this man in my house doesn't seem like such a bad idea after all.

Chapter Three

It's funny, I wouldn't have thought I could share my life and my friends with someone else after what I went through in my divorce. However, as time goes on, Mike just keeps worming his way more and more into my life, and what's more, I seem to be more and more comfortable letting him.

It's a nice weekend in March, and I'm in Liverpool having fun with some friends of mine at an annual event we all attend together. These are my good friends. The ones who know the most about me. The ones who are fully aware of how I met Mike, of how I spent my free time. They know I'm the 'kinky one' of the group, and they enjoy teasing me about how things are changing now that Mike is on the scene. I'll get my revenge. He laps up the fact that they wind me up about it, but I can always turn those tables.

We're sitting at the bar when Eipha asks us all if we want to go out for a meal to this great little Mexican place she's found. Jennifer, Maggie, and Annabella agree, but I explain that I need to wait for Mike, and I have no idea when he'll show up.

"Bring him!" Eipha insists, and the rest of the gang looks at me expectantly.

I smirk back at her. "Eipha, I have one word for you... Pegging..."

Her face lights up with glee. "Fuck, yes!" She's practically rubbing her hands in delight, keen for more details. "Details. I need details!"

I laugh. "You know the way I've been seeing him for a while now? Well he's a filthy one, he likes bum love and being in my knickers. As in wearing my knickers."

Maggie snorts and goes red. "Jesus, Kat. Too much information!"

Jennifer just grins and knocks back her drink.

"This is just making my life right now you, know this?" Eipha laughs.

I shake my head with a grin. "I'm so glad this is working out so well for you!" Just as I'm laughing at the girls' reaction, my phone chirps with a text.

You should come outside.

I chew my lip as I read it.

"Ohh, must be the bum lover! Do we get to meet him?" Eipha asks.

"Go have your meal. I'll meet you in the hotel bar later, if I'm not too busy." I smile as I get up from my seat and head for the main door of the lobby.

I walk out into the cool March evening air and look around the car park. I can't see him, and then I see a figure getting out of what I recognise to be Mike's car. I cross the car park calmly and throw my arms around him when I finally reach him.

"Hello, stranger." I smile at him as he nuzzles into my neck.

"I've missed you," he murmurs against my shoulder.

I stand there for a while, relishing the arms that I have missed for a few days before releasing him and stepping back. I place my hand in his and head back to the hotel's main doors, with him beside me.

We walk into the lift in silence, just casting meaningful looks in each other's direction every few minutes. Just as the lift is arriving on my floor, I look at him.

"The girls asked if we would be back down later. I told them I didn't know, since I would be deep in your ass while you wear my knickers." I smirk and depart the lift, waiting for him to collect himself and follow me.

In a second, he's beside me.

"You don't mind if they know what a little whore you are, do you?" I ask, feigning innocence.

"It's all good." He smiles back. I really have met my match with Mike; the further I push, the more he stands his ground, relishing each challenge to his alpha tendencies.

The door to the room closes and Mike drops down on the bed on his back. I move to the other side of the bed and flop down beside him on my stomach. His hand is instantly on my back, rubbing me soothingly. He knows that just his hands on me is enough to turn me on, even with a gesture as chaste as this one.

"Mmmm, that feels nice," I say, soothed by his touch. His large hands continue to stroke my back. But it isn't enough. I need more, and knowing Mike, he knows exactly what he's doing. I push myself off the bed and watch his face as I slip off my bra, without removing anything else, and throw it in his direction. I grab the tops of my leggings and knickers from underneath my dress and yank them down. I step out of them, leaving them in a pile on the floor, joining Mike back on the bed, face down as I had been before.

Mike's hand returns to my back. His touch is firmer. His hand skims lower on my back, and I know I've affected him as much as he's affecting me. His hand creeps lower, and my dress rides up, exposing my bare backside. He cups my buttocks firmly. I groan and push my ass back against his hand. He grabs my flesh harshly and rolls onto his side, tucking himself in against my side. His hand dips between my legs, and I part them to allow him the access he's seeking.

Instantly, his fingers find my wet cunt and slide between my labia, settling on my clit. His lips touch my bare shoulder, and a low growl ripples over my skin when he finds me already so slick for him.

I lift my head and move towards him. I need to capture his mouth with my own. As soon as my lips touch his, Mike slips a finger inside me. I moan against his mouth as he licks along my lips and penetrates them with his tongue. All day my thoughts have been consumed with anticipation of the night ahead and a desperate desire to feel Mike's touch. It doesn't take long for him to make me lose control. As soon as he slides a second finger inside me, I can't help but clench around him.

When he feels my orgasm subside, he removes his fingers from my pussy and lifts them to his lips, licking them clean of my juices.

"Damn, you taste good!" He smiles, taking exaggerated licks from his fingers. I move on the bed, forcing him to lie on his back again. I indulge myself with a kiss, tasting myself on his lips, then I move again. Before he realises what I'm doing, I turn to face his feet and straddle his head, quickly lowering my pussy towards his face. "Since I taste so good, perhaps you should get a better opportunity to savour me," I tease, just as my cunt makes contact with his nose and mouth.

A muffled groan comes from below me, and his hands suddenly grip my thighs, pulling me against him harshly. His tongue works its way along my pussy, teasing, pushing inside me before returning to my clit. His nose is pressed against my ass, nuzzling against it when he plunges his tongue inside me and pressing into my pussy when he laps at my clit.

It's not long and I'm coming again. My juices coat Mike's face. He knows how wet he gets me and loves feeling it against him. I lean forward and undo the button on his jeans and reach inside to free his rock-hard cock. When my fingers make contact with his skin, another groan vibrates through my sensitive cunt. I press my body against Mike's and take his cock into my greedy mouth.

His right hand disappears from my thigh, and I feel it working my wetness towards my asshole. I moan around Mike's cock, and it pulses in my mouth. I'm here sitting on his face, and still my alpha needs to take some control. His finger now pushes against my ass, seeking entry as his mouth latches around my clit for him to suck on it.

He overloads my senses when his finger slips into my ass and he starts to fuck it. I come again, crying out around his cock as he keeps me impaled on him at both ends of me. I let him fall from my mouth with a pop and grab him tightly in my fist. I give him a hard squeeze.

"Remember who is in control here, slut!" I pant as he continues to work my clit and ass. I dig my nails into his balls roughly and another, louder moan erupts beneath me.

"Oh, you liked that, huh?" I taunt him. He bites on my clit, just enough for me to feel a sharp sting. I moan and grind against him roughly, while slapping his hard cock, reminding him he needs to let it go and give in to me. He rubs the hand he kept on my thigh over me soothingly. I know he is granting me the control I crave. I grind against him and let him lick and finger fuck me to one more orgasm before I finally get off him.

I grab my discarded knickers from the floor, returning to the bed to use them to wipe my juices from his soaked face. I kiss him hard, a silent thank you for the multiple orgasms he's given me so far, and to thank him for his submission.

"Strip," I order when I pry my lips from his. Silently and without complaint, Mike rises from the bed and makes a show of stripping off every last item of clothing. I sit and wait, enjoying the sight of more and more of his amazing skin on display.

When his last item of clothing is discarded, he stands in front of me defiantly, his cock bobbing proudly in front of him. I hold out my hand, dangling my knickers in his direction. "Get these on." I smile.

He glances at the knickers I've been wearing all day and just used to wipe his face. He licks his lips and takes them from me, stepping into them, locking his gaze with mine as he pulls the red lacy panties up his legs, over his thighs, and into place covering his cock, balls, and ass.

I bite my lips, delighting in the sight of Mike's cock straining against my knickers.

"God, I love it when you're a little slut for me," I breathe out. His dick bobs when he hears the word 'slut.' I love the effect it has on him when I call him names like that. There's a real thrill in seeing his head bow slightly and his eyes glaze over in desire. It's the small, seemingly insignificant elements of submission I love the most.

I stand and move towards him, feeling like a big cat after its prey. I give him a wicked grin and lead him to the small table in the room. I line him up near it and push him by the shoulder, indicating that I want him to bend forward over the table.

He complies, leaning forward, his stomach resting against the tabletop, his rear end sticking out behind him. I grab my long silky scarf from the back of the chair and fasten it around one wrist, loop it around the single support in the middle of the table, and fasten it finally to his other wrist. He's now stuck there, bent over the table. My victim, ready to take whatever I desire.

I reach between his legs and rub his cock through the red lace that confines it. A low rumble escapes from Mike at my touch. I smack his backside hard, and then move away from him to where my bag is at the bottom of the wardrobe. I lift out two things: my strap-on, in its harness, and the pair of knickers I wore all day yesterday. I remove my dress, hang it up, enjoying that I can take my time and let him wait, anticipation building within him.

I slip into the strap-on harness, drawing it slowly up my legs as Mike watches from the table. I take my time in securing it in place and adjusting the straps. I then step in front of him, hold my realistic-looking faux cock near his face and demand, "Suck it, whore."

His lips part, and I push the tip of my dick into his mouth. My hand goes to the back of his head as I push the strap-on further towards his throat. When he's like this, I own him, and I don't hesitate to make sure he completely understands that.

I give him a moment to acclimate to me in his mouth

before I start to thrust, my cock pushing a little further in with every stroke.

"Look how pretty you look with my knickers on and my dick in your mouth. Being my filthy little whore suits you so well!" I tease him, and he moans around my dick. I love to take him like this. I love to see him accepting me and feel him resisting me less and less with each penetration of his slutty little mouth.

I give him one final rough thrust, and he gags before I pull out of his mouth. I place my worn knickers under his nose and let him smell them. I want him to know that they have been worn; I know he gets off on it. I'm not sure he's aware that I know, but he soon will be.

"Do you smell that, slut?" I ask.

He looks up at me. "Yes, Miss," he replies.

"You like that, don't you?" I smile.

A slight blush flushes his cheeks and he licks his lips. If I was looking, I know his rock-hard cock would have twitched in appreciation.

"I know you like how my knickers smell after I've worn them, you filthy little deviant. Now, open wide," I command, shoving the balled-up panties at his lips. When he opens his mouth for me, I cram them in, gagging him on them. His eyes are hooded with lust. I can't resist the look on his face. I know he wants more, and to deny him would be cruel.

I walk behind him, grab the lube from the dressing table behind him as I go, pop the lid, and start to make sure my dick is nice and wet for Mike's ass. Normally, I would tease him a little, applying lube to his asshole with my fingers, but this time, I feel the need to be a little bit cruel. I apply a liberal drop to my cock head instead and begin to rub it against his arse, giving a firm push, relentlessly begging entrance.

Tonight, I don't want to tease him. Tonight, I want to be merciless. I don't thrust and tempt him, looking for entry. I demand it. I keep the tip of my cock pressed against his asshole and I push. I keep pressing until, with a loud muffled groan from Mike, my cock slides inside, right up to the fake balls that hang below my fake cock. I don't waste any time, I don't let him adjust; I need to take him hard and rough. I need to possess him. I pull back until the tip of my cock is almost out of his ass before I slide back in to the hilt. More muffled moans sound from Mike. I repeat the tease of almost withdrawing and sinking back in over and over.

The more I hear him enjoying it, the more I feel him raising his arse to meet me, the more it spurs me on, and the more I repeatedly pound deep and hard into him, fucking him like my life depends on it as a frenzy of lust takes over me. A sheen of sweat covers both of us as I keep riding him hard. I always position my strap-on in such a way that it sits almost where a real cock would hang against my body. In doing so, pounding into someone like this always creates a delicious friction through me to my clit. The wave of pleasure starts, my nails dig into his hips, and my thrusts become faster and more erratic, urgent. Soon, I'm crying out as I drive deep into Mike one last time, my own orgasm ripping through me, slickness coating the tops of my thighs because of it.

I remain there for a few minutes, deep in Mike's arse, my knees just about holding me up. I'm distracted when my phone chirps with a message. I slowly ease out of him and step towards my phone. The girls have made it back to the bar and want to know if I'm too busy to come down. I feel like having a little fun with this, so I text back that I'll be down shortly. I grab a butt plug from my bag, add a little lube, and move back to Mike, sliding the plug into his well fucked asshole with relative ease. I move to his head and pull the knickers from his mouth, bending to kiss him hard on the lips. I move back behind him and stoop to his feet.

"Lift your leg," I command, tapping his right ankle. I slip my knickers over Mike's foot and repeat the demand on his left ankle. I stand and slide my knickers up his legs, pulling them into place over his cock and filled arse. I give him a hard smack on the buttocks and untie his hands.

"Come on, get dressed. The girls are back, and we're going to the bar for a drink or two with them."

He straightens. "Like this?" he asks, his hands rubbing over his still rock-hard cock. I look at him and rethink my plan of action just a little. With my own cock still bobbing between my legs, I kneel before him, thighs parted, and dip the front of my knickers to free his cock. I wrap my lips around him and suck him deep into my mouth. He groans, his eyes close, and his head tilts back. His hand grabs the base of his cock firmly, and I let him slip from my mouth again. He begins to fist his hard dick furiously in front of me, and within minutes, he comes hard, shooting his load over my tits. I keep my eyes on his and rub his essence into my skin, over my breasts and stomach, especially my knickers.

"I'll spend the evening knowing that you are wearing my knickers with a fat plug in your arse, and you can spend it knowing that I'm wearing you all over me," I tell him and rise to get dressed. Mike grabs me at the waist as I go past and pulls me against him hard, kissing me forcefully.

"And fucking sexy you look wearing it too," he tells me as he nuzzles into my neck. I nudge him away from me.

"Get ready," I demand and smirk as I watch him tuck

his already-hardening cock back into my knickers and walk towards where his clothes were discarded on the floor..

I doubt we'll stay long in the bar. Both of us are too wound up and ready to have our hands all over each other, but it will make for a very interesting hour or so of foreplay while we do.

Chapter Four

I have been planning this particular adventure for a month now. I need to head to Birmingham on some business, and Mike suggested it would be the perfect opportunity for us to have a little fun.

I'm in my hotel room, waiting for him to arrive. I'm wearing strappy heels, stockings, a silk shift dress, and nothing else. There's a knock at the door, and I open it. When he walks into the room, I can't help but smile. He doesn't know what I have planned for him, but I know he's going to love it.

I walk over to him and kiss him, wrapping my arms around him. I hate admitting it, but it's getting to the point where I miss him when he's not around. But I also know the reason for this visit, and I'm not going to deprive him or myself of it for much longer. I push him back and look at the lust written all over his face.

"Strip," I demand of him.

He smirks at me and pulls his t-shirt over his head slowly, letting me savour his exposed skin more and more as he knows I like to do. He's always told me how much he gets off on admiring my naked form, but I don't think he truly understands just how much I get a kick out of exactly the same thing.

I lick my lips, captivated by the broad chest and shoulders that have been exposed for my visual delights. Mike pauses and looks at me, discarding his t-shirt on the floor beside him. I smirk and shake my head.

"And the rest," I demand. My eyes follow his hands to the top of his jeans, and I wait. I already know he's hard for me. I know he has been before he even walked into the room, but it's the pleasure I get out of this particular tease. Me standing here fully clothed, while he stands naked in front of me, his cock hard. There is a real pleasure for me in knowing I'm the one who got him like that.

He pops the button, undoes the zip, and looks straight at me, almost daring me to say something about what he's going to flash. I look at him and raise an eyebrow, and that's all it takes for him to drop his jeans and boxers to the floor, stepping out of them and his shoes and kicking them all aside.

His hands cover his cock, and he looks at me again. "Is this what you wanted?" he asks.

I cast a glance down at the socks still on his feet. "Everything, slut. Every last item of clothing. And I don't remember saying you could cover yourself with your hands."

His eyes go down to his hands, and then to the floor and his feet. His hands lower, his cock freely pointing upwards when he moves to remove his socks. When he stands straight again, he leaves his hands by his sides. My pussy clenches to see him there, ready for me, and so clearly willing to do whatever I want.

I swallow and take a deep breath. "Get on your hands and knees," I command.

Mike sinks to his knees before me and puts his hands on the floor in front of him. I take the chance to admire his ass in this position; one I fully intend to make good use of later, but until then, I'm going to have a little more fun. I put a foot out in front of him and I tell him to lick it. He glances up at me with heavy-lidded, lust-filled eyes, leaning forward and placing his lips around my big toe as best he can around my shoe, and sucks.

I'm not sure if it's that I have a particular fetish for feet, but there is something intoxicatingly powerful about the sight of a man naked on his hands and knees kissing and sucking on your feet. I watch him, almost hypnotised, every single touch of his on my foot seemingly sent directly to my pussy, making me wet, needy, and wanting so much more. I swap feet and let him lavish the other one with just as much attention as the first.

There's a very specific task I want to achieve with Mike today. He let it slip to me some time ago that he has never been able to come with oral sex. Sure, he's been able to push himself with a hand job, or other elements, to eventually come in a woman's mouth, but never from her mouth directly. Obviously, this is something I want to claim as mine. I want to be the first woman to drive him to climax with just her mouth, so that no matter what happens between us, any time in the future, all blow jobs will remind him of the woman who could. It's a little narcissistic, but I'm a dominant. Claiming firsts just has that appeal, and while I'm usually claiming some firsts in the games I've played in the past, there's a striking freshness to claiming a first of this kind.

I lift my foot from the floor in front of him and push him back.

"Ah-ah-ah!" I scold. "Let's not get carried away, my little slut."

He gives me that look, the one I get when I call him names like 'slut.' I know the effect it has on him and how much he enjoys it.

"Heel." I smirk as I strut past him and head for where my usual bag of tricks is. I grin when I see he's crawling on his hands and knees behind me.

He looks at me, waiting to see what I will pull from the bag. We've talked about a lot of different things he would be willing to try, but I have purposefully not mentioned anything about what I'm going to do this time around.

I lift Mike's favourite lingerie of mine out of the bag. I can see the cogs in his mind moving. He knows this situation well enough to know it couldn't possibly be as simple as me stripping off in front of him and putting it on for him. He understands there will be a catch, and I'm about to tell him what it is.

"Stand," I tell him. I pull a pair of stockings from the pile. I move towards him, circling them around his neck, letting them brush over his skin before using them to pull him closer to me as I kiss him hard and deep, making my lust for him abundantly clear.

"These are for you," I tell him when I pull back from our kiss. He looks at me, and I feel his cock bob between us. He's definitely going to enjoy this. I kneel before him, his cock just inches from my mouth. I wet my lips with my tongue in a move made purely to exaggerate the possibility of the situation. I part the stockings, setting one beside me, and start to carefully open one out between my fingers. I motion for him to lift his foot and step into the stocking, which he does without hesitation. I delight in running my hand over his leg, from ankle to thigh, as I pull the hold-up into position. I smooth it out around his thigh, letting my fingers gently caress the fold of his buttock at the back, my wrist just grazing against his balls as I do.

Mike groans, his eyes close, and his head drops back a fraction. I'm loving every second of blissful torture this seems to be forcing on him. I let my hands slide back down over his stocking-clad leg as I retrieve the other stocking from the floor beside me and begin the same process on his other leg, caressing him softly as I cover him in the sheer material and lace.

As I stand, I see the tip of his cock glisten with precum, and I can't resist taking it in my hand to give it a cleansing lick.

"Fuck," Mike moans. I smile and stand back, returning to the lingerie I had lifted out of the bag. Mike knows what's in store for him now. He watches as I pull the lacy panties from the small pile and unfold them. "You know why I like these?" I ask him.

He shakes his head.

"Because later, they are just neat enough for me to be able to ball them up and put them into your mouth while I fuck your greedy little ass. Can't have the hotel complaining about the noise." I smile and rub the knickers across his lips before I drop to my knees in front of him again and help him into the panties I have, pulling them up and having them straining under the weight of his throbbing cock.

The sight of him in my stockings and knickers has me practically spontaneously combusting. I'm not sure when the game changed, but it did. It used to be that this was all about me giving the pleasure, taking what I wanted and needed in the process. Now, doing all of these things with

Mike makes me just as wanton as he is. The ground is always shifting beneath my feet now, and I'm loving the excitement and the thrill of it all.

I return to the pile I have waiting for him, and I lift my half-cup basque, the one that matches the panties, and I tell him to turn around. I wrap my arms around his waist, taking the liberty of placing small kisses across his back between his shoulder blades as I do.

"Put your arms in," I tell him as I hold the basque out in front of him.

He slips his arms into the straps, and I wrap the garment around him and start to fasten it up the back. When the hooks are all in place, I fasten the attached suspenders to his stockings and then stand back to admire my handy work.

I'm not sure I can describe how it feels to see a man wearing my underwear. Maybe it's the stark contrast between this broad-shouldered, hairy-chested, otherwise alpha man, and the delicate lace and sheer material that surrounds him, or it's knowing that where his hard cock now sits was once pressed firmly against my wet pussy. There's just something about it that makes me feel empowered and incredibly turned on.

I can't help myself. I pounce, driving my lips hard against his, wrapping my arms around his neck. He wraps his arms tightly around my waist, pulling me in against him, pressing me against his hard lace-covered cock. I feel the need in his body. I can read his want and it matches my own, but I'm not ready to let him get what he wants quite so easily. My little game isn't over just yet.

I bend him over and tell him to get on his hands and knees on the bed. I watch as he does, drinking in every movement of his masculine form. I move behind him and slap my hand down hard on his backside. He hisses at the sting and presses back against my hand when I caress his buttock to soothe his burning skin. Before he can settle into the sensation too much, I crack my hand back down on his backside again and caress over the warmed skin once more.

I return to my bag of goodies once again and lift out a large butt plug with a remote control and some lube. I slip the remote into the top of my hold-ups and step back towards Mike's ass. Now I start the real teasing. I smack him hard on the ass again, this time slipping my hand between his legs to cup his balls, also running my hand over his hard shaft. He groans and shifts his hips to try and grind against my hand. Knowing he is so ready for me makes me wet. I know where this is leading, even if he doesn't yet. I need to taste him; it's practically a physical need within me now.

"Look at you grinding against my hand like a common little whore," I mock. "Tell me you're a whore, and I might just let you come."

"I'm a whore, Miss," he breathes.

"Sorry, I think I missed that. What are you?" I say, letting him rut against my hand a little more, rubbing him more firmly, giving him almost enough friction, but not quite.

"I'm your common little whore, Miss," he calls out.

I remove my hand and spank his ass again.

"Indeed you are my little whore, and do you know what happens to whores?" I ask him with an evil smirk.

I roughly pull aside his panties exposing his tight asshole. I pop the top on the lube and apply it to the valley between his buttocks, and using my fingers, liberally rub it around his entrance, teasing it every once in a while by slipping my fingertip in, making sure he is very well slicked up.

"Oh, God..." he moans.

I add a little more lube to my hand and coat the plug with it, then I introduce it to Mike's ass. "That's right, good little whores get taken hard anyway I want," I remind him as I push the plug into him in one slow move. I know what this is doing to him, but I know he'll get off on the relentless penetration. I intend to take him to the brink of desire before I even get my lips around his amazing cock.

I cover his arse again with the sheer material of the panties and give him one last hard smack for good measure, making sure to connect with the base of the plug as I do. The long moan he lets out tells me that I have achieved the level of wanton need in him that I had hoped to. Little does he know, I'm not even remotely done yet.

"Get on your back in the middle of the bed," I demand. Mike does exactly as he's told. He knows what he wants, and he knows I'm going to give him what he needs. "Hands on the headboard."

Once his hands are where they're meant to be, I take great pleasure in removing my dress and revealing to him that I have nothing on but my stockings beneath it. The look of lust and desire on his face is almost enough to make me just straddle him then and there, but I have a prize in mind still, and I intend to collect it.

I approach the bed at his feet and kiss them softly, putting my hands on either side of his legs and slowly creeping up over his stocking-covered skin with a peppering of indulgent kisses. Once I reach the top of his thighs, I cup my mouth over his balls, my hot breath radiating through the thin fabric covering them. Mike's hips rise against my mouth, and I feel his eyes burning into me.

I look up at him and meet his gaze as I pull the knickers down and free his now-engorged cock. I lick from his exposed balls to the head of his dick without breaking eye contact.

"Jesus!" he hisses, and without waiting any further, I sink my mouth over him and take him deep into my throat. His muscles tighten at the sensation. I begin to slowly work my way up and down his shaft, teasing it with my tongue, constantly looking at him, making sure he sees just how much I enjoy having him in my mouth. Just how much I want to taste more of him. Just as his body starts to match my movements with its own, I break my contact with his cock and move to his nipple, laying my naked flesh against his side and wrapping my leg over his.

My half-cup basque has his nipples fully exposed for me, and I waste no time in sucking the closest one into my mouth and lapping at it with my tongue. Mike hisses. I know he's enjoying it; I just need to take him that extra mile. As I suck and nibble on his chest, I reach for the remote control tucked in my stocking and turn it on. A small vibration starts in the plug in Mike's ass, and he groans, his body grinding against thin air.

I tease his other nipple between my finger and thumb, and when I know he's wound up just enough, I move back down his body and take his cock in my mouth again. This time, I'm met by thrusting. He needs release and I fully intend to give it to him. I press the button on the remote again, and the sensations increase within the plug. Again, Mike's hips start to move, meeting my mouth with every lick, pushing back into my throat further and further with each stroke. I lap at him hungrily. I need this now; this is pushing me towards my satisfaction as much as his.

Mike is panting. I know he's close, so I press the remote one last time and set it to the highest vibrations it can manage. I let my hands roam over his thighs and cup his balls again, then move my fingers to the base of the plug, grabbing it through the sheer fabric to start to move it slightly in and out of his ass, fucking him with it, increasing that delicious sensation that only comes from the feeling of having your arsehole fucked.

Suddenly, Mike's hands are in my hair. They push on the back of my head, holding me against him as he thrusts into my mouth in an irregular, spasming rhythm. He's moaning loudly, and suddenly he explodes in my mouth, crying out as he climaxes hard, filling my mouth with his cum, letting me taste every last drop of him. I swallow the first few spurts as they flow down the back of my throat, but I then pull back slightly, letting him finish on my tongue instead. I hold it in my mouth and let him finish, squeezing the last drops from him with my lips then letting his sated dick lie flat against his stomach. I move back up along his side and crush my lips against his.

His tongue enters my mouth, and I know he's tasting himself on my tongue too. He groans and pulls me hard against him, his tongue lapping at mine, savouring how he tastes in my mouth. I've claimed my prize, I press the off button on the plug to still it, and he keeps me drawn tight against him. His lips part from mine, and he licks the last of his taste from them.

"Holy shit, Kitty Kat." He sighs contentedly. I grin and rest my head on his shoulder, my fingers absently fiddling with his chest hair, his warm arms tight around me, and both of us lie there in the blissful bubble we created around us for a while.

Chapter Five

I'm tired by the time I get back to the hotel in Luton. My morning meeting in London had dragged into afternoon. When I open the room door, I hear the shower running and smell Mike's delicious shower gel. I take a deep breath, enjoying the fresh scent before dropping my bag, kicking off my shoes, and stripping off. I creep quietly into the bathroom, unheard by Mike.

He jumps when I pull back the shower curtain and step in to join him under the warm water. He puts his hands up on the wall and allows me the opportunity to run my hands over every inch of his body. I waste no time in rubbing my fingertips over his broad shoulders, placing kisses over the skin that my fingers have touched. I sweep my hand downwards and cup his ass, allowing a soapy finger to slip between his buttocks. Mike groans and his hips move back against my hand.

"Hello, slut." I grin against his back. He turns and envelops me in his arms, capturing my mouth with his for a smouldering kiss. I wrap my arms around his neck and allow myself to melt in against him.

"Long day?" he murmurs against my neck as he nuzzles into it, nibbling on it gently.

"Something like that," I reply.

Mike turns me in his arms so that my back is against his chest. His hands slide over my shoulders and he starts kneading my flesh firmly. I moan in relaxation as he continues to massage my shoulders. I let my hands slip behind me and find his hard cock. I massage him as he massages me.

His mouth makes contact with my left shoulder, and he bites into my skin. I let my head fall to the side, allowing him more access, enjoying the pleasure the pressure of his mouth is stirring in me. I might like to be dominant, but I enjoy it even more when my possessive alpha marks me and claims me; I'm starting to quite enjoy being his.

"Kat!" he warns as I continue to stroke his length in my hands. He moves against me, his need taking over. My own need to stay in control also rises, and I turn to face him.

"On your knees," I tell him. Mike doesn't argue and sinks to his knees in the bottom of the bathtub. I put a foot up on the side of the bath, opening my legs and exposing my pussy to him.

"What are you waiting for?" I ask. Mike grins as he looks up at me, his mouth inching towards my waiting cunt. His tongue laps from my pussy entrance to my clit. I hiss, fisting one hand in his hair, using the other to steady myself against the cool tiled wall.

He slides his hand up my leg from my calf to my thigh and onwards until he reaches my wet sex. His tongue slips along my entrance, parting my labia for his fingers to slip inside. He fucks into me and wraps his lips around my clit again. He works me until I'm on the edge of orgasm. He nips at my clit with his teeth and a climax slams through me like a tidal wave. I shake against Mike's mouth, my legs barely able to keep me up. His hand slips from me and cups my ass with his other, holding me, making sure that my legs don't buckle.

I need to feel him inside me properly; I don't even need to say it. Mike reads the expression on my face and rises to his feet. His lips meet mine again, and he pulls my leg from the side of the bath to hook it around his hip.

He rubs the tip of his cock against my cunt until it finds its home, and he sinks deep inside me in one movement. My head falls back in ecstasy at the sensation of being filled by him so completely. Mike grabs my hips, pulling me tight against him. He then pulls back before fucking me hard.

I wrap my arms around his neck and hold on to him as he begins to pound into me mercilessly. Mike thrusts hard and my back makes contact with the cold tiles. I hiss. He grins and thrusts into me again, forcing me to make contact with the cold wall for a second time.

I run my hands through his hair and pull. "You'll pay for that," I warn, and he growls with another forceful thrust deep inside me. A moan escapes me on the next stroke, and he picks up the pace a little, pushing me for more moans of pleasure to fall from my lips. I involuntarily give him what he's seeking. My cries grow louder and more frequent. He's pushing me towards another orgasm, and I need it.

Quickly, the waves of pleasure take over, my pussy clamps tightly around his cock, and I climax hard. Mike pauses in his thrusts and waits for my orgasm to wane before he goes straight back to thrusting as deep as he had been, his fingers digging into my buttocks as he keeps me needy.

Mike pushes me to two more orgasms before he thrusts into me so deeply that we bump back, resting against the cold tiles again as he fills me with his cum, deep in my cunt, both of us coming hard. When we both recover, his semi-hard cock slips from my soaked sex. I protest at the absence of him. I move off the tiles and press myself against him, manoeuvring myself back under the warm water.

Mike smiles at me, letting me warm my skin.

"Don't you grin at me, slut," I warn him. "Knees now!"

His cock bobs, coming back to life already as he sinks to his knees. I move forward, place a leg back on the side of the bath, and again expose my pussy to him. He instantly leans in, his tongue slipping once again between my labia.

He moans in appreciation. "Your pussy tastes so good full of my cum," he tells me before plunging his tongue back inside me. I let him; I can never get enough of his mouth on me, his hands on me, his cock inside me. He laps greedily, enjoying the mix of his taste and mine from my cunt.

I grab his hair and pull him back off me. We had talked about some of the things he had secretly fantasised about, and I am just about to indulge him with one of them.

"Open your mouth wide," I command. He does as he's told, and using my grip on his hair, I direct him back close to my pussy. I push, and a warm golden stream starts to flow from my pussy. For a second, he jumps back, but the grip I have on his hair doesn't let him move far. A second more and he moves closer, making sure he catches all of the piss flowing from me.

"That's right. Drink it," I command. "Prove what a filthy little boy you are."

I feel his tongue against me again as I continue to empty my bladder over him. His throat convulses, and I know he's drinking everything I'm giving him.

"Close your mouth," I tell him, and the last of my golden flow hits his closed mouth, runs down over his jaw, his neck, and covers his chest, running down over his rock-hard cock.

When my bladder is finally empty, I tug on his hair again. "Tongue," I demand. His tongue comes out from his mouth, and I wipe myself against it, using him to lick me clean. Once I'm satisfied, I pull him back from my cunt, grab a squirt of shower gel and give myself a wash and rinse off, then I step out of the shower, wrapping a towel around me.

"Clean yourself up, you worthless little piss whore. And don't you dare have a wank," I tell him, fastening the towel at my breasts and leaving him in the bathroom to get cleaned up.

Chapter Six

He wanted me to push him further. He wanted to be even more of a little slut for me, but as he stands in front of me now, dressed up completely in feminine things, I can't help but wonder if I have pushed too hard. I look him up and down as he stands here in stockings, suspenders, knickers, bra, a slutty, club-wear-style revealing red dress, and thigh-high PVC hooker boots. When my gaze meets his, I'm struck by the dangerous look of lust veiled in his hooded lids.

I move towards him and back him up against the wall, grinning at the look on his face, and run my hands over his thighs, up under his skirt. I reach inside his knickers and run my hand over the top of his hard dick, finding it slick with precum already.

"You're so wet for me, my little whore," I tease him and crush my mouth against his, needing to taste him with urgency. His arms instantly tighten around me, pulling me tight against him. I wrap my arms around his neck and deepen our kiss, penetrating his mouth forcefully, loving how his broad, manly frame feels against mine covered in lace and sheer fabrics.

Mike runs his hands along my arms until he reaches my hands, then he circles my wrists with his long fingers. He pulls my hands from behind his head and draws them back behind me, forcing my breasts to stick out proudly, pressing harder against his chest.

I part my lips from his for a moment, ready to complain about him restraining my hands, but he distracts me by nuzzling and nibbling on the sweet spot on my neck before I get the chance. I moan at the delicious sensations his mouth on my neck generates, the tension in my reaction ebbing, replaced by need.

Mike manoeuvres us, his mouth alternating between deep, penetrating kisses to harder and harder nips and kisses on my neck and shoulder. He releases my hands and yanks my dress quickly over my head, undoing my bra and sliding it down my arms.

Once I'm standing in just my knickers, he pulls my hands back behind me and fastens them there with my bra.

"What are you doing?" I ask him in alarm. His finger covers my lips to tell me to stay silent, and he turns me so my back is against his chest. His mouth returns to my shoulder, kissing and nipping at my flesh. His hands, now free from their task of restraining me, move to my breasts. Mike cups my tits firmly in both hands and kneads my flesh, his forefingers and thumbs finding my already hard nipples and rolling them between his digits.

This goes against everything I usually do in play. It ruins the sense of control I like to maintain, and yet because it's Mike, and because of the trust I have in him, the need I have for more of him in this moment far outweighs any need I have to control this situation. He presses his erection against my bound hands as he nuzzles my neck and gropes my tits, and I indulge in a little groping of my own. I wrap my hands around his cock as best I can and move them up and down his length.

Mike groans, and my efforts are rewarded with a harsh bite on my shoulder and a cruel twist of my nipples.

"Ah! Ah!" he warns. "You've been teasing me long enough, Kitty Kat. It's payback time," he announces in a breathless whisper against my ear. A shiver runs through me. The feeling of his hot breath over my skin makes me need him even more than I already do. He moves away from behind me and turns me to face him. "Turn around," he demands, and I find myself willingly turning to face him. "Kneel for me, little Kat," he says softly and kisses the tip of my nose, and I sink to my knees in front of him. The expression on his face when he looks down at me tells me everything I need to know. I know what he's thinking, what he expects from me, and just how turned on he is by the prospect.

He hitches up the hem of his dress, pulls down the front of his lacy panties, and lets his cock spring free at me. Instinctively, I lick and bite at my lips and look up at him. Mike uses his thumb to push down on the length of his cock and point it directly to my mouth.

"Suck it," he tells me.

I open my mouth and take him inside, instantly tasting his precum on my tongue. I moan around the head of his cock as I greedily lap at him. Mike fists his hand in my hair and pushes my mouth down on him further.

I run my tongue over the underside of his length and look up at him. A low groan escapes him and spurs me on. I push further, taking even more of him between my wet lips. Mike's hips twitch, and his grip on my hair tightens.

"You keep looking at me like that, Kitty Kat, and I'll not be able to stop myself from fucking that beautiful face of yours," he warns me breathlessly.

His words fan the flames of my desire. I want him, no I *need* him to push me; I want him to take over. I widen my mouth and push him as far in as my gag reflex allows, holding still when I find my limit and breathing through my nose until it passes.

"Jesus!" he hisses. Unable to resist anymore, Mike pulls back and thrusts into my mouth. He groans a low rumble as he sets a fast pace of claiming my mouth, pushing further and further towards my throat.

My knickers are soaked, and my nipples are painfully hard. I need more of this than I ever imagined possible. It's not until my eyes are wet from fighting the need to gag that Mike pulls his rock-hard and swollen cock from my lips.

"Enough! Get up," he groans and helps to pull me back to my feet. He leads me to the bed and tells me to get my knees onto the bed and move forward. Once he is happy with where I am, he gives me a shove and I fall flat on my face. An instant later, he's between my legs, pushing them further apart, exposing me to him.

He yanks the crotch of my knickers roughly out of the way and sinks into my drenched cunt in one hard stroke. I moan loudly at his abrupt penetration, my voice croaky from the abuse my throat has just taken. Mike begins fucking me with ruthless precision. He pulls out almost completely before forcing himself back in even deeper. It isn't long until my pussy starts to tighten, and that feeling of impending orgasm creeps low in my stomach. Seconds later, on another deep hard thrust, I cry out as an incredible climax consumes me.

As my greedy little cunt pauses in its tight grip on

Mike's dick, he continues his routine of almost withdrawing, followed by a deep hard thrust. My hips instinctively lift against his movements as best they can with my arms behind my back. A second and third orgasm slam into me in quick succession, and suddenly, Mike pulls out.

Before I have the time to protest, his fingers find my juices and start rubbing them up towards my arsehole, making it just as slick as the rest of me. The head of Mike's cock pushes against my ass. I catch my breath as I try to relax, already sure of what's coming next.

Mike puts his weight into pushing into my arse, and after a moment of pressure, he penetrates me once again. I cry out at the sensation, the feeling scorching every nerve ending in my body and sizzling right through to my clit. He's slow and gentle in his movements, but he's taken me so utterly that I'm on a complete overload of sensations. I feel completely possessed by Mike, lying here face down on the bed, my arms tied behind me, and my ass being stretched and filled so deliciously. My little bubble is burst when he leans against me and breathes across my ear.

"What do you call me, Kat?" he whispers.

It takes me a few moments to register what he's asking me while he's pushing deeper into my ass with every stroke.

"What do you call me?" he asks a little more loudly.

"A whore," I answer with a moan as he thrusts back into me slowly.

"And if you're being fucked in the arse by the whore, what does that make you?"

I groan at where this conversation is going. I know what he's doing. It's the game I've played on him. It's the words and the taunting I've done. I just never realised how potent they were on the receiving end.

"What am I, Kat?" he insists, the pace of his thrusts picking up.

"A whore," I moan.

"What does that make you?" he asks again.

"The whore's whore," I cry out as another orgasm starts to wash over me.

"Fuck." The almost plea-like outburst comes from behind me as my body clenches and releases with the climax.

A soft sheen of sweat has settled over my body. I feel wrung out, and yet so in need of even more from Mike. As my senses clear a little, he picks up the pace.

"You have a whore in a dress deep in your ass, Kitty Kat," he teases me breathlessly.

A groan rumbles through me; I'm turned on like I've never been before, and this man is the reason. This experience is fast becoming the most liberating thing I've ever done. His breathing hitches, and I feel him pulse in my ass. I know just how close he is. I can feel another climax building in me, and I'm overcome with the urgency to have him join me.

"Oh, fuck," I moan. "Fill me. Make me your whore."

My words become both our undoing; he bucks against my ass in one hard movement, a guttural moan resonating through him. I clamp around him and cry out as I come once more. Mike jerks inside me as he comes hard, deep in my ass. Moments pass as we both recover from the shattering climaxes that have quaked through us.

He pulls his semi-erect cock slowly from my arse and drops down onto the bed beside me. His hand goes to my wrists, and my bra is untied, freeing me from my binds. I grumble as the stiffness in my shoulders becomes apparent, moving against Mike to be on my side against him. My hand comes down over his chest and I rub my fingers lazily over his chest hair. When I glance up at him, his lips come down hard on mine.

"Thank you," he murmurs against my lips.

"What for?" I ask him.

"Your trust," he replies. "And you have no idea how sexy it is to think of my cum deep inside you." He grins and possesses my mouth once more. I surrender to him, silently acknowledging the trust I have in him, and how right he is about being claimed.

Chapter Seven

Mike has been teasing me with some sort of surprise for the entire fortnight that he had to be in the States for business. He had told me a few days ago; it was something he'd had since just before he left.

He walks in, scoops me up, and kisses me hard. "I have fucking missed you!" he murmurs against my neck, peppering it with kisses. "I need to be inside you, Kitty Kat."

I can't help but agree with the way he's thinking. It's been too long. I missed him. I missed how his hands feel on my naked skin, and how his mouth feels on mine, and most importantly, how perfectly he fits inside me to rock me to climax.

I smile and nuzzle into his chest. "I thought you had something for me," I say with a grin.

Mike flashes a grin back, and with a raised eyebrow, replies, "Oh, you know I do!" He flexes his hip against me so I feel his hard cock through his jeans.

I roll my eyes. "That wasn't what I meant, and you

know it. But I'll take it!" I say, grabbing his hand and pulling him upstairs behind me.

Mike wastes no time in pulling me against him again when we reach my bedroom. He surrounds me in his arms, plants his lips on mine, and pulls me so tight against him it's almost like he's trying to fuse us together.

He grabs the hem of my t-shirt, tugging it over my head and throwing it across the room. I go for his shirt, and he pulls away from me, holding up a finger, silently telling me to wait. He kicks off his shoes, removes his socks, and looks at me through hooded eyelids.

"Strip for me," he says, his eyes roaming over my already exposed flesh. I turn my back to him and grab the waistband of my leggings, peeling them down over my ass, revealing a lacy little red thong. When my leggings reach the floor, I kick them to the side. I turn back to face him and undo my bra, letting my breasts spill from the cups as it slides down my arms. I throw that to the side, and it lands with my discarded leggings. I let my hands skim over my breasts, dropping them to my sides; I'm purposely not taking off my knickers yet. Not until he's lost more of his clothing.

"Now what?" I ask innocently.

Mike's primal look almost sets me on fire with the intensity of his gaze. "Oh, you'll lose those soon enough," he warns with a devilish glint in his eyes.

I take his unspoken challenge and move towards him. I grab the waist of his jeans and unbutton them. I then pull down the zipper and hook my thumbs in, sliding Mike's boxers and jeans down. He steps out of them, and I bend to move them out of the way. His cock bobs beside my head, and I look up at him, never breaking eye contact as I wrap my lips around the head of his cock and take him deep into my mouth.

A loud gasp comes from Mike as I suck on his length. "Fuck!" he hisses. His hand naturally goes to the back of my head. He sighs in satisfaction when he is able to push me and sink further into my mouth.

When he finds my gag point, he groans and pulls out of my mouth with a pop. "I have to have you," he says, and I move to undo the buttons of his shirt before running my hands underneath and pushing it off his shoulders and down his arms.

I'm about to lean in to kiss him again when something on his chest catches my eye. On his left pec, under a tuft of chest hair that's barely there compared to the rest, is a tattoo. In a little black outline, looking almost sexy, is a cat. Underneath it in a delicate script is, "My Kitty Kat."

I stare at it, lifting my fingers over it without actually making contact.

"Do you like it?" he asks anxiously.

I look up at him. "You have my name on your skin forever?"

"Unless you really piss me off, and I go for laser removal." He grins.

I'm astounded at the gesture he's made; he's left me lost for words for a change.

"Do you like it?" he asks, his arms around me again.

"Yes." I say, trying not to overthink the 'what ifs.' "I love it," I admit.

"You're so fond of marking me, Kitten, I thought I'd make it permanent."

My lips crash into his and I claim his mouth. I'm moved by his actions, unable to express myself, so I show him how I feel. He pulls me hard against him, amplifying my passion with his own. His hands slide down my sides and he rips my thong off, pulling it from my body in tattered pieces. He lifts me, and I hook my legs around his hips, and my arms around his neck. He sinks me down on his cock until he is fully sheathed in my wet cunt.

He thrusts into me slowly and I start to feel overwhelmed by the sensations and the emotions of the moment. I find myself needy and feeling emotionally raw. When Mike thrusts in deep, words unexpectedly fall from my lips on a sigh.

"Fuck, I love you," I breathe. I don't get the chance to overthink what I've just uttered. Mike's thrusts pick up the pace and I'm lost to the sensations he's generating within me.

"I feel just the same about you. Move in with me," he pants, pausing his thrusts. I move against him, and he holds me still. "Move in with me," he murmurs against my lips. Again, I try to get the friction I need, and he holds me tighter still. "Kat," he growls.

"This is sexual blackmail!" I glare at him.

"I love you. Move in with me," he says again.

"Fine," I agree, desperate to feel him moving against me.

"Yes?" he asks.

"Yes! Okay, yes!" I exclaim.

We land on the bed a moment later, and he begins thrusting into me again, racing me to the climax I have been so desperate for.

—

A few weeks later, after talking it all over, Mike brings his stuff over and he moves into my house with me. Things are still evolving. I enjoy the control as much as I ever did. But I'm also learning that the take part can be just as much fun as the give.

THE END

About the Author

Dee Lish is an Irish author who loves to indulge her imagination with some filthy stories. She's been publishing under other pen names since 2014, but in 2023 returned to her erotic roots.

She likes to spend what little spare time she has binge watching her favourite shows, reading, and making messes and memories with her two children.

You can follow her on social media, or join her newsletter for all the latest naughtiness!

Also by Dee Lish

Succumb to Me Series

The Mistress

The Ponygirl

The Handled

The Punished

The Corrupted

The Student

One Handed Reads Series

Teased

Owned

Seduced

Tempted

Desired

Unexpected

* * *

Dee Lish also writes romance as Leighann Duncan

www.authorleighannduncan.co.uk